I0734356

Suburban Heathens

ALSO BY ELLEN LANSKY

Harmonic Convergence

Golden Jeep

Suburban Heathens

A Novel by

Ellen Lansky

BRIGHT
HORSE
BOOKS

Copyright © 2018 by Ellen Lansky
All rights reserved.
Printed in the United States of America

Brighthorse Books
13202 N River Drive
Omaha, NE 68112
brighthorsebooks.com

ISBN: 978-1-944467-15-9

Author Photo © Michèle Steinwald
Cover Photo © valentinrussanov

For permission to reproduce selections from this book, contact the editors at info@brighthorsebooks.com. For information about Brighthorse Books and the Brighthorse Prize, visit us on the web at brighthorsebooks.com.

This book is a work of fiction. The characters, incidents, and dialogue are drawn from the author's imagination and are not to be construed as real. Any resemblance to actual events or persons, living or dead, is entirely coincidental.

Brighthorse books are distributed to the trade through Ingram Book Group and its distribution partners. For more information, go to https://ipage. ingramcontent.com/ipage/li001.jsp. For information about Brighthorse Books, go to brighthorsebooks.com. For information about the Brighthorse Prize, go to https://brighthorsebooks.submittable.com/submit.

Gotta make a move to a town that's right for me.
— from "Funkytown," Lipps, Inc.,
by Steven Greenberg

"Oh God," he thought, "what a hard job I picked for myself!"
—Franz Kafka, "The Metamorphosis"

1

THE TV WAS CHAINED to the snack machine, and car magazines and an ashtray littered the coffee table. Nothing interesting was happening in the waiting room. Rickie Lynn Jackson was not in a hospital, where Code Blue teams might rush by, but in a body shop on Lake Street, in a Minneapolis neighborhood that was marooned between the Mississippi River and the Chain of Lakes.

Two nights earlier, some drunk bastard had plowed into a whole line of cars parked on the street. Sirens and noise on Park Avenue had awakened the entire household. Rickie and her housemates had gone outside to see that Rickie's car, in the middle, had been done in: back bumper torn off, right side smashed in, front end buried in the car in front of it. Within an hour, the cars had been towed away and everybody had gone back to bed.

Now, as she sat on a metal folding chair in the body shop waiting room, Rickie Lynn Jackson flicked her thumbnail at the edge of her car insurance card. She made some calculations. It was the summer of 1985, and Rickie was twenty-four years old. She'd just finished a master's degree in English at SUNY-Binghamton, a medium-sized university in New York's Southern Tier. She'd left Binghamton a few days after she learned that her friend Michael Haik had died of AIDS. The news of Michael's death had hit Rickie with the force of a sledgehammer in the stockyards, and she was still feeling like she could collapse in a heap at any moment. Her friend Deborah Walker had also finished her graduate work at Binghamton, and she had already planned to move back to Minneapolis, her hometown, to take a job in a consulting firm, buy a duplex, and be closer to her family and new girlfriend. When Deborah heard about the death of Michael Haik, she convinced Rickie to come to Minneapolis, live in the new duplex, and work in her brother's grocery store until she was ready to find a teaching job, get a PhD, or go to work in a downtown office and scribble poems during coffee breaks and lunch hours. The duplex and the grocery-store job were helping Rickie feel the ground under her feet again, but now she had on her hands a wrecked heart and a demolished car.

The car was a 1978 Chevy Chevette, white with red plaid interior and not much more than a stick shift, a heater, and an AM radio. Her parents had bought it at the end of the summer before her junior year in high school. Her brother was away at college, and Rickie's parents figured it was easier to get her a car and let her drive herself to and from school, sports practices, and games. Back then, the Chevette wasn't fancy, and it wasn't fast, but it was brand new. When Rickie went off to college, the car went with her. The car was hers in the same way that Alice, the dog, belonged to Rickie's mom, Annie. Just like Alice, the Chevette had picked its favorite. In the body shop that summer day on Lake Street in Minneapolis, Rickie felt worse about the Chevette than she'd felt when Alice had died of dog-cancer.

Rickie shifted in the hard chair. The day was warm, and the seat of her jeans was sticking to the warm metal seat of the folding chair. She'd been out drinking the night of the Park Avenue Demo Derby, and it was just pure luck that she'd parked the Chevette and gone inside to bed before she herself sideswiped a row of cars and got hauled off to detox or jail. She was thinking it might be some kind of sign from the universe if she walked out of the body shop with a big fat insurance check, but that kind of luck didn't seem likely.

She put her ankle up on her knee and bent over it to stretch her aching ass. She inhaled and exhaled and figured that even if she did get a check, she'd have to call her parents to tell them to cancel the insurance because some drunk driver had sideswiped the Chevette, and it was beyond repair. It wasn't her fault, but it kind of was. Her mom would give her that "Have you been drinking?" look, which Rickie could feel even over the phone, and even if she hadn't been drinking, she could tell that Annie didn't believe her because more times than not, the true answer to Annie's question was usually "Yes" with some kind of qualifier like "But I wasn't driving" or "But not that much." If Rickie said, "No," as she usually did, they'd both know that she was saying no because Annie wanted to hear it, lie or not. It was complicated.

It was all complicated: the recent week she'd spent at her childhood home in Shawnee Mission, Kansas, why she'd left Binghamton in such a rush, and why she was now rushing off to join Deborah in Minneapolis. All anybody could talk about was AIDS, AIDS, AIDS. Just before she'd left Shawnee Mission, a kid down the street had told her this joke:

"Hey, Rickie," the kid said. "You know the worst thing about having AIDS?"

Rickie stared in stunned stupidity. "No," she said.

"Having to tell your parents that you're Haitian!"

Rickie wanted to grab the kid by the front of his shirt and shake him. Instead, she stepped back and said, "You don't even know what you're talking about."

The kid cocked his head. "Rickie," he said. "Why are you still a tomboy?"

The next day, Rickie left for Deborah Walker's duplex on Park Avenue in Minneapolis.

•

Outside the body shop, the claims adjuster was assessing the damages. Rickie had arrived before the claims adjuster and had gone back to see for herself.

"That your car?" a mechanic had asked. A patch on his shirt said "Dutch."

"Yes," Rickie said. The car's front end, now detached from the rear end of the car in front of it on Park Avenue, was smashed in like a boxer's nose. Before she'd left the house that morning, Deborah had told her to get rid of it if the front end was bad.

"Hmmm," Dutch said. "Here. Pop the hood."

Rickie shifted her gaze from the smashed front end, opened the driver's side door, and pulled the hood release.

"Don't look too good," said Dutch. "See those fresh little seams? The frame's cracked."

"Well, what does that mean?"

"It means," Dutch said. "That this one's ready for the bone-yard." He let the hood drop.

•

"Rickie Lynn Jackson?" said a voice as the Personnel Only door swung into the waiting room.

Rickie put her feet on the floor and pushed back in the folding chair. "Yes?"

The claims adjuster, with a stringy comb-over, crooked aviator frames, and brown suit, did not exactly smirk, but he didn't smile either. "Let me put it to you like this," he said.

•

From the body shop, Rickie walked back to Deborah Walker's duplex, three blocks south of Lake Street on Park Avenue. Park Avenue used to be swanky, but it was not swanky at all in the mid-80s. Even so, Deborah was the only person Rickie knew who had the smarts and the cash to buy real estate. She joined the people of color, hippies, anarchists, punk rockers, artists, and fags and dykes in the neighborhood and bought herself a domicile that had been a single-family mansion and then a rooming house and then a duplex and now was a cross between an artists' colony and a dorm.

"Hey, Rickie Lynn," she called. "What did they say?"

"It's wrecked," she said and figured Deborah would approve. "Totaled."

As she approached the front steps, she could see Deborah on the porch. Deborah was taller and bigger than Rickie, an average-sized ex-high-school-girl-athlete. Deborah had the solid build of a butterfly swimmer, a power forward, or a catcher, and though she had never, ever played sports, she had the swagger of a jock. She was wearing tan boots, jeans, a tool belt, and a white T-shirt. A red bandana covered her hair. She nodded as she lifted up a window screen and peered through it.

"That's what I figured," Deborah Walker said as she fixed her gaze on Rickie. The two of them were friends at first sight in the dorm at SUNY-Binghamton. Both had a parent who was Jewish. Deborah's dad was black and a physician; Rickie's dad was a secular Jew and a physician. Deborah's mom was a practicing Jew and a social worker; Rickie's mom was a white lapsed-Catholic psychiatrist from Nebraska. Deborah knew what she was doing, and they both knew it. She inhaled, and Rickie held her breath.

"If the front end's been rattled, your car wouldn't run the same anyway," she said. "Even if they fixed it."

Rickie felt sunk inside.

Deborah Walker put down the screen. "I know you loved that car, Rickie Lynn," she said. "But you're better off without it."

•

TEN YEARS PASSED. RICKIE Lynn Jackson was still living in Deborah Walker's house, now a duplex with Rickie in the bottom unit and Deborah and her girlfriend on top. The pet Chevette with the loyal heart and the bad front end had gone from the body shop's back lot to the boneyard. Michael Haik, Rickie's friend, collaborator, and muse was still dead, and so were dozens of guys Michael's age and her age who never made it to forty or thirty-four or even thirty, some of them, because AIDS killed them fast and young between the mid-80s and early 90s. As the 80s ended, the AIDS cocktails slowed the death derby, and the millennium approached, Annie, Rickie's mother, was killed instantly when a driver, too busy to stop at a red light, took a sharp right turn into the crosswalk and ran her into the ground. "Senseless," everybody said. Rickie's dad, CJ, still lived in Shawnee Mission, Kansas, but CJ stopped driving and sold his car after Annie's death.

Not long after the deaths of Michael Haik and the pet Chevette, Rickie got a job teaching composition at the downtown Minneapolis community college that was a few miles north on Park Avenue, and though she actually could have bought herself a new car if she'd really wanted one, she got used to taking the bus or riding her bike. She quit drinking and started going to AA before she killed herself or somebody else. By now, after the deaths of Michael Haik and all those other young and handsome men, the pet Chevette, and her doctor-mom, it was as if she'd never really been a driver anyway. That part of her life went to the boneyard, too.

In fact, she was just about to walk outside to the backyard and chat with Deborah Walker about the latest project in the Park Avenue duplex when the phone in the kitchen rang. She let the answering machine pick it up, expecting a telemarketer or somebody calling for Deborah, who was now a consultant. Instead, it was Tom, her brother, calling from New Zealand, where he was working on a marketing project. He was speaking pitched, sharp words that sounded like a telegram echoing in a tin can.

"Rickie," said Tom. "Bad news. It's CJ. His heart. I'm in New Zealand, so I can't make it. Will you please go home?"

2

By 1995, the Shawnee Mission suburbs of Rickie Lynn Jackson's childhood and teen years had expanded south into what used to be the country. Strip malls, corporate enclaves, and fancy shopping centers had sprung up in landscapes that used to be marked in soybean fields, herds of longhorn cattle, and occasional single oil rigs—hopeful as big metal birds dipping their beaks for a worm. The houses in her old neighborhood were well maintained and the same as ever. Developments to the south boasted huge houses with state-of-the-art sports facilities, top-notch schools, and high-end shops.

To the north, though, in the not-ever-very-nice section of Kansas City, Kansas, KU Medical Center, never fancy in the first place, was now like a building in hospice care—on a morphine drip until it passed, after an interminable decrepitude, into its long-awaited final demise. The waiting room did not have a TV. It still had end tables and lamps with round light bulbs and lampshades. On this already hot morning, the humidity was getting to everything. The lampshade next to Rickie was sagging on its frame.

Before she and CJ had left CJ's apartment that morning, Rickie had found a late-70s-era KU football T-shirt in the back of the hall closet. It still fit, and so did the running shorts she'd worn with that T-shirt at the end of the 70s and was still wearing now: different shorts, same size. She scrunched her toes inside her running shoes, which were sticky because she wasn't wearing socks. She figured she'd go

14

for a run later in the day, after the sun went down and at least some of the heavy heat went with it.

Rickie and CJ had arrived at 7:50 for an eight a.m. appointment, and the nurse with a clipboard had called CJ back at 8:15.

"Charles, is it?" the nurse asked as she led CJ and Rickie to the scale. She was wearing a pink smock. She could have been an art teacher, a nanny, an occupational therapy aide, a matron in a madhouse.

"Yes," CJ said. He was a physician and could have been wearing a white coat. Instead, he was a small, gray-looking old Jewish guy in various shades of blue: light-blue button-down shirt, navy chinos, indigo comfort mocs.

Rickie looked at him in surprise. In all her many experiences in the hospital with her dad, CJ had always been polite but insistent about the fact that he was a doctor: a *macher*, not just some old blue Jewish guy named Charles. Nobody but strangers called him Charles. "Actually," Rickie said. "It's Dr. Jackson."

The nurse puckered. "Let's get your weight, Dr. Jackson," she said.

A few minutes later, a knock on the door signaled the entrance of a tall man. He wore big glasses, a white shirt and tie, and navy slacks. Rickie noticed he was wearing black slip-on shoes with rubber soles, like CJ's comfort mocs, but he'd squashed down the backs so they were more like the clogs that the nurses and surgeons preferred. He was not wearing a white coat. A short white coat meant medical student, and a long white coat meant resident. A long white coat with an embroidered name meant big shot professor honcho *macher* person. This guy simply had a stethoscope draped around his neck. He came in and shook hands with CJ.

"How do you do?" he asked in slightly British cadence. He said his name, but all Rickie caught was Edward, his first name. Edward started asking CJ the usual medical history questions. CJ described his recent trip to Saint Louis, where he'd had a couple of terrifying episodes of shortness of breath while he was visiting relatives: his son Tom and Tom's wife, Nancy; his niece, Becky, Becky's partner, Sue, and their son, Charlie. Usually, CJ was excessive with detail, and Rickie was expecting him to describe the barbeque dinner that they'd eaten in Becky's backyard on the Fourth of July. Instead, he used the word *dyspnea*.

Rickie gaped at CJ and then at Edward, the doctor resident *macher* nurse man. Edward nodded. Then CJ went on, describing more symptoms, and said it again. Dyspnea. Edward then used it and pronounced it in the exact same way—each as if he were sort of half-swallowing the word as it came out of his mouth. CJ nodded.

In that moment, it was clear to Rickie that CJ had just given Edward some sort of exam. It was also clear to Rickie that Edward had passed, which was saying something given the fact that CJ generally did not trust doctors of color who were from somewhere else. In fact, most doctors who were not Jewish he did not trust. "What's your specialty? Internal medicine?"

Edward smiled and shrugged. "I don't know yet," he said. "I'm a medical student."

"Oh," said CJ. He sat back a little bit and eased up. "Really? What year? Third? Fourth?"

"First year," Edward said. He shook his head and gave a laugh. "This is my first history." He stood up. "Dr. Ostergaard will be in shortly."

Before CJ and Rickie could size up the first-year medical

student, who'd had to do his first history ever with a retired physician who was accompanied by a family member with just enough knowledge to be dangerous, someone knocked. In walked Dr. Ostergaard, a not-young and not-old man who looked like a doctor version of Garrison Keillor: tall, with short hair and round brown glasses. Dr. Garrison Keillor Ostergaard came in and asked all the same questions, not even bothering to look at Edward the med student's careful and copious notes. He sent CJ along for a chest X-ray.

While waiting on folding chairs in the hall for CJ to have a chest X-ray, Rickie and her doctor-father, now a patient, evaluated the clinical scene.

"The medical student was earnest, but the Garrison Keillor doctor wasn't so great," Rickie said.

"The med student tried real hard."

"That other guy kept wiping his nose with his fingers."

"He was picking his fingernails, too. He seemed nervous," replied CJ. He exhaled. "He was a *putz*."

"Nobody took your pulse."

"Medicine's going to hell in a handbasket."

"Let's open a clinic," Rickie said. "I've got scrubs. All I need is a stethoscope."

"No, you don't. I've got one. I've got a doctor bag for you, too, and you can use my license."

•

THE CHEST X-RAY TURNED up nothing immediately alarming or noticeable, and CJ got the last appointment for a stress test and an echocardiogram. He seemed downcast, and when he pushed through the door to the waiting room, it seemed to Rickie that the color had drained out of the scene, as if the filters had been switched to black-and-white.

"What happened?" Rickie tried.

"Well," CJ said. "There was some irregularity."

"What does that mean?"

"*Ver vaist*," he said. In Yiddish, this meant "who knows." It also meant, "No use talking about it."

"*Ver vaist*, OK," Rickie said with rising tones. "But what exactly is wrong?"

"We don't know quite yet," CJ said. He seemed to deflate and sink a little bit. Rickie could hear it in his exhale, in the tone of his voice. Then CJ continued. "I was hoping to live another twenty years."

Rickie tried not to gape. CJ was at that moment sixty-two years old. Nobody on the Jackson side of the family had rebounded from heart disease; her grandparents hadn't even made it to seventy. To Rickie, it sounded like CJ was asking for eternal life. "What happens next?" she said at last.

"They want me to have an angiogram."

Rickie felt a familiar rising panic. She was sure that CJ was not being straight about the heart problem. "Well, what exactly is it, this angiogram?"

He shrugged. "You go to the cardiac lab, and they thread a catheter through a vein in your hip. They inject some dye and take a look at your veins and arteries and your heart to see what's *farflootchkied* and what's not."

"I'll go with you," she said. "I mean, I can drive you." She'd arrived late at the airport, and the car rental company was fresh out of the economy car she'd requested, but there were plenty of SUVs on the lot. The attendant at the rental desk had given Rickie a wink and an upgrade to a royal blue Chevy Blazer. It was a vehicle she'd only ever seen driven by lesbians with gelled hair and severely ironed shirts. If her housemate Deborah had been there to see Rickie open the door and climb in, she'd have laughed her ass off, first. Then she'd have said what she always said about cars: "Fancy coffin. Better off without it."

"It's a routine procedure," CJ insisted.

"It can't be that routine," Rickie said. She crunched her toes inside her sneakers. She inhaled sharply through her nose and then exhaled. It wasn't exactly relaxing, but it was better than screaming her head off. She inhaled again. "Anyway, Mom always said you should never go to the doctor alone when it's something serious."

CJ exhaled and gave a tiny smile. "All right, dolly," he said. "You'll take me in the morning, and then we'll go to lunch."

•

THE NEXT DAY, STILL in her ancient KU football T-shirt and her shorts, same as ever, Rickie looked up from the 1960s vintage linoleum floor in the waiting room when through the swinging doors walked a burly man in blue scrubs. The man's belly pushed at his V-neck scrub shirt, sweaty around the edges. At the end of a thick, hairy arm, he extended his hand. In Rickie's mind's television screen appeared John Belushi doing that yellow-and-black bee sketch on *Saturday Night Live*. CJ always called him Belushki.

"My name's Dr. Anton," Belushki said. "Your dad is up in the OR now. Here's what we learned. In the course of the CPR, he incurred a broken rib."

"He incurred a broken rib?" Rickie said as she struggled out of the chair—half-hauled up by Belushki's handshake. Repeating Belushki's odd phrase felt sickening. "From CPR?"

"Yes," Belushki continued. "It's a common outcome with CPR, and in fact, in most cases of successful CPR, ribs are broken. It's not good, but it's better than the alternative."

"Why was he even having CPR?" Rickie felt like she'd

been socked in the solar plexus. She inhaled through her nose and managed not to pitch forward.

"His heart stopped. But now there's another problem," Belushki said, and he rubbed his palms. "The rib fracture lacerated your dad's liver and ruptured his spleen."

Now Rickie's heart leaped halfway up her throat. The tips of her ears burned. She flexed her hands and wished she'd brought along Deborah, a work buddy, an old high school friend, anybody who'd stand next to her, grip her elbow, squeeze her fingers. Rickie's voice shook when she spoke. "Lacerated liver," she squeaked. She hated this shaking voice. She sounded like she was about to start bawling, but really, she did not feel like crying at all. Now well into the arid zone of sheer fear and panic, she was beyond crying. "Ruptured spleen? Did they stop the bleeding?"

Belushki held out his palms. "They're working on it. But I need your permission for them to remove your dad's spleen."

Rickie gulped. She'd gotten a B+ in college anatomy, and she recalled that the spleen wasn't a life-or-death organ. Belushki and his crew could take it out, and CJ wouldn't be that much worse for the wear and tear. Still, when CJ woke up, he'd have to deal with his still-bad heart, a broken rib, and no spleen.

Rickie took another deep breath. She wished her mom were here. She could just see Annie straight-arming her way through those swinging doors, marching all the way back into the cardiac lab with CJ to make sure those cardiologists and residents and medical students and nurses knew what they were doing. If something had gone wrong, Annie would have known how to fix it. She'd have reached in and squeezed CJ's heart in perfect lub-dub iambic rhythm, no busted ribs, no smashed spleen. He would have opened his eyes and smiled at her.

Belushki moved his feet and raised his palms. "OK to take the spleen?"

Rickie took one more breath. "OK," she said and nodded at Belushki. She took a step backward as Belushki brushed past, leaving what felt like a sweaty chemical streak on her arm. She was trying to wipe her arm with the bottom of her T-shirt when there came another gentle *tap tap* at the door.

"Come in," Rickie said. She looked up and saw a different doctor in blue scrubs.

"I'm Dr. Shapiro," he said.

Rickie nodded and felt a flush of relief as she sized up Shapiro's black curly hair and brown eyes. And the nose: a thin, sharp rise, just like the one she had before she'd busted hers in a high school softball infield drill error. CJ would appreciate Belushki's energy, but Rickie felt certain that CJ would be a lot happier in the midst of this catastrophe if at least one if his doctors were a Jew. Rickie waited a beat for Shapiro to continue.

"Is there heart disease?" Shapiro began. "In the family history?"

Rickie held up her palms, nodded, and gave Shapiro a *ver vaist* shrug. Shapiro returned a half-hearted smile and said he had to get back.

With a dull ache in her stomach, Rickie sat down in the uncomfortable waiting room chair and blinked hard. The family was flush with heart disease. CJ's parents, Sol and Leah Jackson, had both dropped dead of a heart attacks before Rickie or Tom were even born. Then CJ's older brother, Kenny, had high blood pressure that had wrecked his kidneys. He'd *plotzed* in a hospital in Buffalo, New York five years ago. Two years ago, CJ's oldest brother Marty had a massive heart attack that killed him instantly in the parking lot outside the grocery store in Syracuse. His other older brother, Jimmy, was still alive in Rochester, New York, but it didn't seem likely that Jimmy had escaped the time-bomb ticker.

Rickie extended her legs, flexed her feet, and looked around. There she was, a lone island in a waiting room populated by groups of strangers. They had Walkmans, books and magazines, bags of snacks, cans of Coke, boxes of Kleenex. One person had stashed a tightly rolled sleeping bag under a chair. Stuffed into a small backpack, Rickie had her wallet, the keys to the Blazer, and the copy of *Love Medicine* that she'd already read twice. People around her had brought comfort food or drinks to this waiting room. She had a comfort book, and that would be enough. Or so she'd thought when she'd dropped off CJ and parked that blue Chevy Blazer in the short term lot. Now, after what should have been a routine procedure to fix CJ's damaged heart, there was instead another family catastrophe.

3

THE CABLE TV STORE on College Boulevard in Leawood, Kansas could have been a bank, some kind of clinic, or a small, expensive electronics outlet. Rickie Lynn Jackson pushed through the front door and paused. Leawood made her nervous.

Back in the late 60s, when her parents were buying their first house in the Shawnee Mission suburbs, Leawood had restrictive covenants pertaining to chain link fences and dogs and had only recently rescinded the ones pertaining to Jews. Rickie's family had a dog and a Jewish dad, so they moved to Prairie Village, near the Jewish country club and the grocery store with the biggest kosher section in town. Now, in 1995, Leawood had sprawled past the freeway. On the freeway's far side, a brand new Jewish Community Center, replete with an adjacent assisted living community, an updated satellite campus of Menorah Medical Center, and a bright, new deli had taken hold. This new cable TV store was located on the eastern edge of the Jewish neighborhood, the suburban *shtetl*, in a development that had been a soybean field not that long ago.

A young woman with black spiky hair, red round glasses, and pale white skin approached her. Around her neck was a lanyard with a company ID badge attached.

"Hi," she said. "How can I help you?"

Rickie gave her what she hoped was her best charming smile. In her hands was the open but unused cable TV box belonging to her father, Charles Joseph Jackson, MD. Dr.

23

Jackson was currently in intensive care downtown at KU Medical Center, and nobody was sure he'd make it off life support. Rickie needed this young woman with the spiky hair to take back the box, shut off the service, and not charge any sort of disconnecting fee or penalty.

"Hi," Rickie said. She looked at the cable person's badge. It said her name was Lauren. If she were Deborah Walker, she would have looked at that badge and said, "Hi, Lauren." Lauren would have cancelled the cable service in no time flat, and they'd have set a coffee date at the deli before she left the store. Rickie had it in her to pick up people, but not like this.

She nodded at the cable box and said, "I've got my dad's cable box here. He's never used it, and I need to return it and discontinue the service. Can you help me with it? Please?"

Lauren's bright smile dimmed. "Let me take you up to one of the service agents behind the counter over here," she said. "This way."

Rickie followed Lauren and set the box on the counter.

"Dan," Lauren said to a white guy behind the counter. "She needs to discontinue her service."

Dan looked like the kind of guy who did not particularly like working in this cable store in a strip mall on College Boulevard near the suburban *shtetl*. Here was Dan, stuck with this Lauren and her glasses and hair and skin, and there was Rickie, a half-Jewish lesbian jock tomboy in an old T-shirt she'd bought in the mall across State Line Road, where Dan, behind the counter, probably not gay or Jewish and not strapping, either, was wishing he was working in the kiosk just off the escalators near the fountains.

"Actually," Rickie said. "It's my dad's. He never even attached this cable box to his TV, and now he's in the hospital, so I'd like to discontinue the service for him, please." She was trying not to rush it, and she left out the part about her mom being killed in a car accident and her dad being horribly depressed and neglecting things like unwanted cable TV service, but she could feel Dan recoil as the words ticked out of her mouth, dropping like little rabbit pellets on the counter.

"What's the account number?" Dan asked.

"Let's see," Rickie said. She opened the box and pushed a letter from the cable company across the counter. "This letter has his name, address, and account number on it." She paused, met Dan's implacable gaze, and continued. "It's one of those letters saying that they'd disconnect the service unless my dad called a number before a certain date. He never called, but he didn't want it." She paused again and felt she needed to push it, even though she could practically hear Deborah Walker telling her to take it easy. "That doesn't sound like very good customer service to me."

Dan flared his nostrils, took the letter, and tapped the keyboard. "Charles Joseph Jackson?" he asked.

"Yes," Rickie said. "CJ Jackson is my dad."

"OK. I'll need to see a POA document."

Dan was looking for a specific document, one that Rickie Lynn Jackson knew she did not have. Even so, she rummaged in her bag and extracted an official-looking document and pushed it across the counter. "I'm the successor trustee," she said.

Dan looked at the document and frowned. "This isn't it. Your dad will have to give permission to cancel this service," he said. "Can we call him?"

Rickie's ears reddened. "He's downtown in the Cardiac Intensive Care Unit at KU Medical Center," she said, now with tones that shook and rose with her reddening ears. "With a ventilator down his throat. He can't talk. He can't write."

Dan sighed. He looked at Lauren and then at a different guy down the counter. "Tony," he said. "Can you help with this?"

Tony came over. He had light brown skin and floppy black hair and was wearing a black shirt and black jeans. Dan repeated his version of Rickie's story. Rickie looked at Tony, who shook his hair. Tony didn't roll his eyes or wink or do anything that might make Rickie feel like he thought the whole thing was stupid, but Rickie had this feeling that if she calmed down and just stood there long enough and did not look pissed off or sound pissed off or even think about being pissed off, Tony would close the account.

Tony listened and nodded at "rolled over," "never activated," and "intensive care." He kept his eyes on the screen and didn't look at anybody. For a tiny hair's breadth of a second, he exhaled and pressed his lips together. Then he gave the keyboard a couple of resolute keystrokes. Somewhere under the counter, a printer chugged. He extracted a document pushed it across the counter to Rickie.

"OK," Tony said to the countertop. "Discontinued."

"Really? Discontinued? That's it?"

"That's it," Tony said, with no eye contact.

"How did you code it?" Lauren wanted to know.

Tony looked at the screen. "Deceased," he said. For the tiniest split second, he looked at Rickie. "He's not going to reactivate the cable service, right?"

Rickie gaped, inhaled, held her breath. Her eyeballs were springing out of her head. They were dangling from her eye sockets on stretched-out coils. Deceased: this was it.

"No," Rickie said and exhaled at last. She couldn't tell if this Tony was kidding, serious, nonchalant, or sadistic. "He's not going to reactivate it."

"Better make sure of it," Lauren said with a laugh. Dan and Tony snapped looks at her, and she closed her mouth.

"OK, then," Dan said as Tony moved back down the counter and disappeared behind a door. He corralled the cable box and the empty carton, the cords trailing like streamers, ribbons, snakes. "That should do it."

"Yes, thanks," Rickie said. She gathered up her papers and tried not to look like a person who was about to run out of the store.

Outside, the parking lot was bordered by split rails left over from the time when this area was marked only by gravel roads, wheat and soybean fields, and vestigial herds of longhorn cattle. Rickie stood there for a long moment, smelling the warm miasma of asphalt from the well-maintained roads: pesticides, gas, and lawnmower exhaust from the well-maintained green lawns, and a whiff of chlorine from the nearby, brand-new waterpark. It was the smell of poison, the smell of home.

4

Mounted on the wall in Cosentino's, a grocery and deli on College Boulevard in Leawood, was a buffalo head. Still sporting its horns and great shaggy brown mane, it gazed over the long deli case that featured salmon croquettes, grilled chicken breasts, tuna salad with navy beans, minestrone, matzoh ball soup, chopped liver, and pasta salad; over the people in tennis and jogging outfits finding unusual imported grocery items on baker's racks and putting them into shopping baskets, over the small tables of parents with kids, of single people reading newspapers, over the long table of well-groomed and nicely dressed old people, Jews from the nearby senior community near Menorah Hospital, walking distance: CJ's neighbors and friends. The buffalo head, implacable, took in the scene. It rested its limpid glass eyes on Rickie Lynn Jackson, who was writing in a notebook halfway between the *alte kackers* and the parents, jocks, and entrepreneurs. Rickie looked up and caught the buffalo's eye.

Right before she'd awakened that morning, she had been dreaming that she and CJ were walking into her duplex on Park Avenue in Minneapolis. Something was wrong. A black-and-brown dog whimpered in a kennel. The bathroom door was not fully open and not fully closed. Rickie pushed open the door and looked in. The bathtub was nearly full, and at the bottom of it was a young woman. She was dead. Rickie stood there for a moment. Could she be revived? Could she and CJ somehow haul her out of the tub and do CPR? Could they resuscitate her? Who was she? In the dream, Rickie

28

understood the young woman, dead, to be her sister, but she also understood that in real life, she did not have a sister. She had a brother, Tom. CJ had a sister, Eileen, who had died not in a bathtub but from cancer. Eileen was twenty-two years old: the age of this drowned sister in the bathtub in the Park Avenue duplex. In her dream, Rickie Jackson felt a flush of panic clutch her stomach. She knew she should do something, try to save the sister, call for help, something. She couldn't or didn't move, and neither did CJ.

The dream jolted her awake, and she pushed her feet down into the sleeping bag she'd thrown on top of the daybed in CJ's tiny den. In the sleeping bag she'd found stowed in the hall closet at CJ's apartment, Rickie didn't feel entirely disoriented when she woke up on the day after CJ's cardio-catastrophe, just after a dream about the dead sister who was now, in dreamland, her dead sister, her dead aunt, or perhaps herself. She shook off the dream but not the sense of an emergency. CJ was in the hospital, and there was no telling when he'd get out.

She tried to imagine what it must be like for him, waking up in a hospital room instead of his own bed at home. She figured it must be the same feeling a person got when he woke up for the first time in a college dorm, a lunatic asylum, a cancer unit, a senior living community, an Indian mission.

•

Now she was sitting in Cosentino's, trying to reconstruct the dream beneath the gaze of the buffalo. It once again seemed strange to Rickie that a Jewish community, replete with a grocery/deli that was a mix of Italian and Jewish, would expand to Leawood, of all places. Maybe founders of the deli and the temple and the JCC had followed the tracks of dozens of other, previously fleeing Jews, including Rickie

Lynn Jackson's Jewish grandmother and great uncles. They all hopped on a train from Grand Central, stepped off to rest in the middle of the country, and stayed. Maybe the Cosentino's people also started in New York and stopped here when they found a suburban village of Jews. Maybe they'd packed up their fine groceries and deli items and belongings, piled in, and driven West in a blue Chevy Blazer. The buffalo head gave the joint what somebody must have thought was local credibility: Plains realness.

•

THE BUFFALO EYED RICKIE as she shut her notebook, got up from her table at Cosentino's, and walked outside. All around her were counties and creeks and parks and schools and streets named after Indians: Sagamore, Cherokee, Wenonga, Shawnee, Tonganoxie. She was remembering that on one of Annie's days off during a hot and boring Kansas summer, Annie had taken Tom and Rickie on a tour of the Shawnee Indian Mission. Rickie got into the Blazer and took the same path through the old neighborhood at 99th Street and then several more miles to West 53rd Street and a peculiar dead end.

The grounds of the Shawnee Indian Mission looked like a park until the buildings came into view. Back in the 70s, the complex looked like a school or a hospital, but not like Rickie's elementary school (Trailwood) or Tom's junior high (Indian Creek) or CJ and Annie's hospital (KU Medical Center). It looked like the kind of school or hospital that made people stay there, like it or not.

She spotted an official Kansas Historical Society sign marking the site and the parking lot, and she wheeled the Blazer into a parking spot. She sat in the driver's seat for a minute and recalled that the last time she'd been here, her mom had explained to her and her brother that the purpose of the Indian Mission was to round up Indian kids, take them away from their families, and put them in this place where they'd learn English and a trade. Tom and Rickie considered the pros and cons of a school where you went to live with no parents and whether it would or would not be fun. Tom said he'd rather go to school and then go home. Rickie thought it would be much more fun to be sent to live with the Indian families out on the plains, living in teepees and racing ponies and hunting buffalo.

Rickie stepped out of the Chevy Blazer and followed the signs to a building that could have been a correctional facility, a school, or a hospital.

Inside, the person at the ticket window introduced herself as the historian-on-duty. She sold Rickie a ticket and said that it was a quiet day in the Mission because the Civil War re-enactors weren't due for another two weeks. The grounds were open, but the building's exhibits were closed

"What are they re-enacting?" Rickie asked. She stood there for a second, casting back in her memory. She snagged the Missouri Compromise of 1820 and the Kansas-Nebraska Act, but nothing about nearby battles of the Civil War.

"Battle of Westport," the historian told her. "It happened just across State Line, not far from where you are standing."

Rickie nodded. She'd never heard of the Battle of Westport. For her, Westport was a strip of dive bars, the Bijou theater, a few restaurants, and a joint called the Silver Fox that was, behind its unprepossessing and unmarked front, a gay disco. When she was in high school, people she knew from her part-time job at KU Medical Center had taken her to the Silver Fox in Westport, sneaking her past the bouncer in a pack of pharmacists, grad students, nurses, and lab techs who knew what they were doing and showed her how to act as if she did, too.

"Thanks," she said.

"What brings you here today?" the historian asked pleasantly. "Visiting?"

Rickie held up her palms. "Kind of. I live in Minneapolis now, but my dad is in the hospital at KU Med Center, so I'm here." She looked around the foyer. "I grew up in Shawnee Mission. I think I've been here before. Probably on a school field trip."

"Well, how about that?" she said. "Welcome back."

A tiny bed pushed up against a closed door caught Rickie's eye. "Those beds are so small," she observed. "Were the kids sick? Or undernourished? Is that why the beds are so small?"

The historian pressed her lips together. "The children helped grow, harvest, and prepare all the food. There was a laundry and a bakery, an outdoor kitchen, and a blacksmith shop. The Mission was almost entirely self-sufficient." Rickie nodded. The historian was just doing her job, but to Rickie, the description sounded just like a slave plantation or a concentration camp.

Not long ago, she and Deborah had gone on a one-day trip the the US Holocaust Memorial Museum in Washington, DC with a group from Deborah's mom's synagogue. At the beginning of the tour, each person got a passport with the name of somebody who'd been sent to a camp. At the time, she couldn't quite articulate why this passport chafed her. She and Deborah both felt that the passport smacked of inauthenticity and then rolled their eyes at their own Culture Wars theory-riven read of everything in sight.

Now, in the Shawnee Indian Mission that depended on the ritual reenactment of the Battle of Westport, Rickie understood the passport as a similar kind of re-enactment. She could go through the tour in Washington, DC, far away from the place where the Holocaust actually happened, and re-enact the person's experience, minus the death in the gas chamber, which turned out to have been the fate of Rickie's person. Rickie whispered to Deborah that if the museum tour was meant to be realistic or authentic in some way, then there should be a selection followed by a march to a replica of a gas chamber, replete with stone soap and fake shower heads. Somebody could figure out a way to replicate the sound and smell of Zyklon-B without actually asphyxiating people. Deborah put her finger to her lips and walked on ahead of Rickie until they reached the cattle car.

Usually, there were always lines at the big attractions. On the day of their whirlwind tour, the cattle car stood there, doors open. Nobody was waiting in line or even nearby. Rickie opened her mouth to complain to Deborah that a real Holocaust cattle car would not have doors open on both sides. It would be one way on and one way out. She said nothing and instead breathed in sharply through her nose, the way she used to do before she went in the hog barns at the Nebraska State Fair. Then Rickie and Deborah walked in to the cattle car together.

Rickie was expecting to feel overwhelmed by smells: sweat, vomit, piss, shit. She was expecting the car to reek of fear, confusion, rage, despair, even after half a century and a move across the ocean to this nice, new museum in Washington, DC. The air felt thick, and she was expecting her sinuses to fill and clog, but they didn't. Instead, what she mostly felt was foreboding, a remnant of the doom that the packed-in Jews had felt in Europe, as if a tapeworm had pierced her shoe and her sole and was wending its way through her body, aiming for her heart and lungs. She looked at Deborah who was blinking and blinking. Without even thinking about it, they grabbed hands and jumped out the far side of the car. Neither spoke until they'd passed through the replica of the gate to Auschwitz: *Arbeit Macht Frei.*

•

SHE THANKED THE HISTORIAN, gave a vague wave, and pushed open the door of the air-conditioned museum. She thought about the historian and her focus on self-sufficiency. It seemed to her that "self-sufficient" was a euphemism, a rationale, for kidnapping and abuse back then. The Indian Mission tried to make the kids strangers to their parents and families and culture, suspicious of each other and probably everybody else around them.

When she was a kid, growing up in a development not too far from here and not too far removed from what was still farmland and before that had been Indian Territory, she'd been sent to become a self-sufficient kid in a Montessori program at a Catholic school not far from KU medical center where Annie was an intern and then a resident. Both Rickie and Tom had attended the Montessori from the moment they were potty trained until it was time to start kindergarten. She did not recall either CJ or Annie talking about Montessori as a good or bad thing. Annie knew the nun who ran the program; it was safe and convenient, and for Annie, that was that. Even so, Rickie always felt that she'd benefitted from the overall Montessori pedagogy and worldview: work, cooking, cleaning, folding laundry, staying busy, getting stuff done. When it was time for her to start kindergarten, she walked there by herself for the afternoon session. Sometimes she felt a little bit scared or lonely, but most of the time she liked being able to do things for herself. She didn't exactly feel like a stranger in her house or at her new school, but later she wondered if she'd taken the self-sufficient part of the philosophy a little too far.

•

OUTSIDE, THE HEAT HUNG on her like a hair shirt. On her way to the Chevy Blazer in the parking lot, she looked around at the semi-restored barn and blacksmith shop. They could easily be picked up and moved or perhaps just easily replicated in a new section at Worlds of Fun, the big amusement park off the freeway that looped from downtown to the southern suburbs of Shawnee Mission. She opened the door of the Blazer and sat down on the steaming driver's seat. She turned the ignition and cranked up the air conditioning. As soon as the air conditioner had driven out enough of the trapped heat, she shut the car door, shifted gears, and headed toward KU Medical Center to check on her spleenless, heartshook dad, trapped on a ventilator: not in the least bit self-sufficient and at this point, barely even alive.

5

"THERE YOU ARE," THE nurse at the desk said when Rickie arrived. "Has anybody talked to you about Dr. Jackson's code status?"

"To me? About code status? As in Code Blue?" Rickie said. She felt a thrill of sharp, confusing panic. The nurse's "There you are" sounded to her like an accusation, a sizing-up, a scolding. The nurse thought she was a bad daughter, and Rickie was sure that the nurse was right.

The nurse pressed her lips together and then smiled. "Yes," she said. "Your dad will know what this is about. When you talk to him, keep it short, so that he can nod or shake his head to give you yes or no answers."

Rickie nodded, walked down the hall to CJ's room, and paused. She was thinking that this was a kind of selection: not exactly the same as "this way to forced labor and that way to the gas chamber," but not exactly different, either. Tom would have been helpful with this conversation, but he was in New Zealand, probably wishing he had better information about CJ's condition. He probably felt like a bad son.

Rickie paused outside CJ's room. She decided it would be best to call Deborah Walker before she started asking CJ life-and-death questions. There was a phone on the wall among the ICU equipment, but it seemed wrong to stand next to CJ's hospital bed and talk loudly above the noise of the venti-lator about code status. Even if CJ could hear her, he wouldn't be able to say anything anyway. Rickie found a pay phone at the end of the hall and used her long-distance discount plan number to call Deborah Walker.

"What's going on?" Deborah said.

"Let's see," Rickie said. "CJ is still on a ventilator and unconscious as far as I can tell. The nurse just asked me to talk to him about his code status, which means she wants him to say that he does not want to be resuscitated. She wants him to select himself for death. I feel like Dr. Mengele!"

Deborah let Rickie finish. "That doesn't sound promising," she said at last. "I mean, do you think he's ready to *plotz*?"

"I don't know," Rickie said, and she rocked up on her toes as she always did when she was perplexed. "When I was with him at that doctor visit, he said he was hoping to live another twenty years. I know it sounds impossible, but still."

"OK," Deborah said, and Rickie could hear her nod and raise her palm, which she did when she was ready to take action. "Here's what you do. Ask him just straight out if he's ready to die. Ask him if he wants the doctors and nurses to take all emergency measures to resusitate him if he crashes."

"Is that one question or two?"

"Two," she said. "Ask him two questions. First, ask him, 'Are you ready to die?' Then ask him, 'Do you want the emergency measures?' He's intubated, right? So ask him to squeeze your finger. Once for yes. Twice for no. Got it?"

"Got it," Rickie said. "Thanks. I'll call you later."

She strode toward CJ's room, or his chamber, his cell: all glass walls and monitors. She stood in the doorway, which wasn't really a doorway but a space created by a drawn curtain. There was CJ in the hospital bed, white-on-white: white hair, white eyebrows, white skin, white sheets. His eyelids were closed and streaky, as if he'd been socked. The ventilator huffed and thunked.

"CJ," Rickie called. She took two steps toward her father

on the huffing, thunking hospital bed. "Hey. How are you feeling?"

The bruised eyelids fluttered, and Rickie leaned over the side rail and took CJ's hand—the one not crisscrossed with tape and hooked up to the IV.

"CJ," Rickie said. "It's Rickie. I want to ask you a couple of important questions, OK?" She was trying to keep her voice at an even, calm pitch, but she sounded breathless, shook. She could hear it, her own emergency pitch. She recognized it from other, equally shaky conversations: trying to explain how the Chevette had been smashed to bits by a drunk driver in Minneapolis; trying to explain that her friend had just died from AIDS after having asked, in shaky tones, a few months earlier, what her dad might know about lesions and rashes, about pneumonia, about diarrhea. Her parents, being doctors themselves, knew about the giving and getting of bad news related to health and sickness, and dinner table banter was always open and lively in the Jackson house, but conversations about gay poets and AIDS were something else. Rickie had told them that Michael was her best friend, that he was gay, that he kept getting sick. Annie said, in her usual way, which was blunt to the point of being mean sometimes, that it sounded like AIDS. CJ agreed. "Especially if he's a *fagel*," he added. Rickie rolled her eyes, exhaled through her nose, and left the table. That was the end of the conversation.

CJ's eyelids fluttered again and then opened. At first, his eyes were as blank as a walleye, but as he blinked once, twice, they began to take on color.

"Hey, CJ," Rickie said carefully. "Um, I'm not really sure how to say this, but the nurse said I should just ask you."

Even with the ventilator mask and tube, CJ looked at Rickie with the same considering, measuring look she'd often seen when she or Tom put an interesting question or quizzical comment to him. Rickie had gotten that look when he'd asked CJ if he thought Annie knew what had hit her when that car took that hard right turn and ran her over in a pedestrian crosswalk.

As the thunking ventilator raised his chest, CJ raised his eyebrows and gave an almost imperceptible nod.

Rickie leaned forward. She swallowed hard and tried to smile at CJ. "OK," she said. "So, first, are you ready to die? Squeeze once for no and twice for yes."

CJ turned his head toward Rickie and squeezed once.

"OK, so no, right?" Rickie said. "That's a no."

CJ blinked. He gave another, single tiny squeeze.

"OK," Rickie continued. "No. So then here's the next one. Do you want them to take all emergency measures to resuscitate you if you crash?"

CJ didn't hesitate. His squeezes were weak, but there were two of them.

"No and yes," Rickie said. "Yes to every possible intervention if you crash, and no, you're not ready to die, right?"

CJ squeezed twice. Rickie's palm felt sweaty, but she kept her grip on CJ's hand. Just then, the nurse came in.

"If you'll just step out for a little bit," the nurse said.

Rickie squeezed CJ's hand one more time and patted his arm. The ventilator thunked CJ's chest once, twice. The bruised eyelids came down.

As she gazed at her dad, Rickie felt a mixture of relief and panic. CJ was not ready to die, but to Rickie, CJ's condition was as grave as the Chevette with the cracked frame at the body shop on Lake Street: ready for the boneyard. A wrecked car could be parted out and then crunched up and recycled. A wrecked person was supposed to go home and die or have full-time care from a spouse or family member. By Rickie's calculations, she was the likeliest caretaking person. The spouse was dead, and other family members were not near enough for full-time care, and even when Tom got back from New Zealand, she'd be on summer break and he would not. She saw the options: she could hop in the Blazer, drive it all the way back to Minneapolis, and leave it on Park Avenue for some drunk bastard to smash to smithereens. She could change her name to Roxanne and deny that she'd ever rented a Chevy Blazer or drove around the southern suburbs of Shawnee Mission, Kansas. The other option was that that Rickie would stay in her sleeping bag in CJ's den until further notice.

6

AFTER THE DAY HAD clamped its pressing embrace of heat on everything in sight and was now easing off a bit, it was a perfect time for a bike ride: hot but not smothering, with plenty of daylight. From CJ's apartment, she took the elevator to the garage to see if Tom's old ten-speed was still in the bike corral.

The last time she'd visited during warm weather, she'd taken the bike to the Schwinn dealer in Prairie Village. The bike tech was happy to see an authentic Schwinn Varsity ten-speed, candy apple red, in decent condition. The tech adjusted the brakes, checked the derailleur, lubed the chain, and set the seat so that Rickie could actually ride the thing, She took it for a spin before she returned it to the bike corral, locked it to a rack, and replaced the tarp that had preserved it like a body in a peat bog. She peeled back the tarp, and there it was: a little dusty and soft in the tires, but otherwise ready to ride.

She stood over the bike's crossbar, and it barely grazed her crotch. As she stood over the bike, she recalled the scene at the bike shop when she'd gotten her first Schwinn Varsity ten-speed. She and Tom had both saved up a hundred bucks, the price of a ten-speed at the time, and Annie and CJ came along to supervise the purchases. On the way to the store, Tom was lecturing everybody about being able to stand over the bar without racking your balls.

"That includes you," Tom said to Rickie. "Even if you don't have balls, you still have to stand over the crossbar."

Rickie said, "Shut up," but she knew Tom was right.

41

About the first thing out of the bike salesman's mouth was, "Stand over the crossbar." Tom swung his over the crossbar of a candy apple red Schwinn Varsity and did not rack his balls.

Rickie's transaction was not so easy. She wanted an orange Varsity, but when the salesman wheeled out the adult size bike, she had to lean the bike over to swing her leg over the frame, and then she had to stand on tiptoes, leaning on one foot.

"That's too big," Annie said flatly.

"It is not," Rickie insisted.

The salesman, a young guy in a tracksuit and a tiny brimmed cap that said, "Campagnolo" in a fancy script, nodded in silence and took a step back. "Let's try this one," he said. He pulled out a bike that was orange and a ten-speed, but it was tiny. Rickie had already declared that she had not saved up a hundred bucks to spend on a kid-size bike. She knew she might not be tall enough yet for an adult-size bike, but she felt that she was too old for a kid-size bike. It would be a total humiliation.

"Just try it," Tom urged.

Rickie swung over leg over what looked to her like an impossibly tiny little toy version of a ten-speed. She put her feet flat on the floor, and the bike barely grazed the seam of her jeans.

"That's the right fit," the salesman said. He'd taken two steps away from Rickie.

"Is that the one you want?" Tom asked.

"Tom," Annie warned.

Rickie felt her ears burn. "I do not want kid-size," she said. Her voice trembled.

The salesman paused a second and then he stepped forward. "Listen," he said to Rickie. He touched the handlebars and she looked at him. "It's not just for kids. Lots of women buy this size bike. It just depends on how tall you are."

Rickie was not sure that she wanted to be one of the women who bought this tiny little bike. She knew she was not a tall person and never had been. In all the photos CJ had taken of her and Tom, the top of her head was usually at the level of his shoulder or sometimes the bottom of his earlobe. Tom was not tall, but he was not short, either. Annie was the same way. CJ was short and always had been. He was always talking about the fact that he had to play JV soccer in high school because he was so short. Whenever Rickie was too short for something—going on a ride at an amusement park or standing over a bike frame when she was old enough for an adult-size bike but not tall enough, CJ or Annie or both of them would say, "You come by it honestly," as if that was supposed to make her feel better. She wanted to throw the ridiculous tiny orange bike to the ground and walk out of the store.

Annie said, "Why don't you and Tom just take the bikes for a ride?"

"Take a test ride," CJ added.

Tom said, "Let's go. Just see what you think."

Of course, everybody thought that Tom's red bike was perfect for him and Rickie's orange bike was perfect for her. The orange bike was easy to mount and dismount, and once she was on it, the pedaling and gear shifting were smooth.

When they returned from the test ride, the worst happened. Tom rolled his bike into the shop and said, "It's perfect."

Rickie rolled the orange bike into the shop and felt her chin wiggle the way it did just before she started crying. She knew she would burst into tears if she looked at any family member, so she stared at the tile floor, streaked here and there with black marks from tires. In the aching pit of her stomach, she knew the options, and they were stark: go ahead and buy the idiotic kid-size bike, or refuse to buy an idiotic kid-size bike and end up with no ten-speed at all.

CJ said he'd pay for both the bikes now and take the money from their saving accounts later. Annie said that the orange bike was just fine, and Tom agreed. Rickie felt like bawling.

As she wheeled Tom's candy apple red Varsity out of the bike corral, she tried to piece together the history of her orange ten-speed. The humiliation and distress couldn't have lasted that long because she'd ridden that tiny thing all through the summer before ninth grade and in all decent weather throughout ninth grade. Tom got his driver's license in the summer after Rickie finished ninth grade, and he said he was done with his ten-speed. She stood over Tom's red Varsity on tippy-toes the night before the neighborhood garage sale. The next day, some short kid in junior high paid twenty-five dollars in cash for the orange bike and rode it up the block and out of sight.

•

ON THIS WARM BUT not-too-hot early evening in Shawnee Mission, Kansas, she rolled Tom's bike to the air pump near the car wash in the underground garage. She filled the tires and doused the chain with the squirt bottle of chain lube that somebody had left near the pump. Then she pushed the bike up the ramp through the big door that the attendant raised when he saw her coming.

Rickie headed out of the parking lot for College Boulevard. She figured she'd ride up to Johnson County Community College, JuCo, where she and Tom and sometimes she and her old boyfriend, Bill DuBois, played racquetball on the outdoor courts back in the late 70s. When she was a kid, nobody had ever ridden bikes out to JuCo—partly because teenagers drove, always, and partly because it was not that much fun to ride up and down hills in a thick wet blanket of humidity and heat.

As she started up the first hill, she was glad that the derailleur worked and she could shift the gears. The hill wasn't steep enough to require stand-up pumping on the pedals, but it did demand some force on the pedals. Her usual routes in Minneapolis were mostly flat, and the muscles in her hips and ass gave a sizzle. Whenever she told people she'd grown up in Kansas, people asked her if she'd ever seen mountains or even hills before. She always shrugged. There was no use explaining that the part of Kansas she knew was rolling hills; the flat wheat fields were mostly straight out west.

As she rolled to a stop at the first intersection, she caught her breath paused on the wide shoulder of College Boulevard. After another big inhale, she decided she'd take a look at those racquetball courts at JuCo and then continue east to the softball complex where she'd practiced and played games and tournaments on her high school team and summer teams. When she was in high school, her varsity team had taken a bus out to the complex after school every day. The bus ride seemed to go on forever, but Rickie figured it couldn't be more than ten miles. In Minneapolis, she rode more than ten miles a day just going to and from work.

The light changed, and the gears slipped when Rickie took off. She managed to sit down, quickly, on the sticky vinyl saddle. The bike wobbled, but she stayed on it and did not rack her balls.

"Shit," she yelled, giving it the full-on Kansas twang so that what came out of her mouth sounded like *she-it*. She jiggled the gear shift, and the chain found its groove. The wind was picking up on College Boulevard, and daylight was starting to dwindle. The lights at the softball complex lit the fields better than daylight, but College Boulevard was lit for cars with headlights and not for lightless ten-speeds. Rickie coasted a second. Then she made a wide U-turn and headed back to CJ's apartment. She coasted down the last hill, and the attendant opened the garage doors for her so she could roll right into the garage and put the old bike back under its tarp.

The garage doors were still open, so she walked up the ramp to the parking lot. When Tom and Rickie were growing up in their big suburban house in Shawnee Mission, the kids in their Prairie Village neighborhood used to play hide-and-seek or flashlight tag when the wide Western summer night sky thickened with grays and blues. Now with the sun's glare gone, the air was the texture of slightly sweaty skin. Above her, the sky was high and by now laced with heat lightning. The cicadas took up their electronic hum.

When she was a teenager, she and the other kids used to go for drives at this time of night. They'd pile in somebody's car and head south, past the strip malls and the car dealer-ships, under the Interstate, and beyond the motels and fast food chains and office parks to the country. They'd stop at a liquor store for strong beer and booze if they were lucky enough to pass for twenty-one or a convenience store for 3.2 percent beer if they were only lucky enough to pass for eigh-teen. Then they'd head south toward Louisburg on Highway 69, where a group of kids swore they'd seen a group of Devil Worshippers, or southwest past Olathe toward Paola and Osawatomie, where rumor had it there were Devil Worship-pers and crazy people at the lunatic asylum.

The Kansas State Mental Hospital at Osawatomie, about

forty miles south of Shawnee Mission, sat on a hill like a warden. The Gothic-style main building laid its gaze on the little town of Osawatomie and up over the rolling wheat fields, right into Shawnee Mission. Rickie's parents didn't work full-time at Osawatomie, but they were down there often enough on consultations, and she and Tom often went along for the ride. Rickie had never seen lunatics or Devil Worshippers or anything more than worn-out farm houses with dead cars and farm equipment—not even a bonfire but a little old grill where people who looked like they were having a family reunion were roasting hot dogs or marshmallows. Even so, in Binghamton, New York, her friends who were wearing black, reading Foucault, and doing theory couldn't believe Rickie's luck: a panopticon practically in her own backyard.

•

SHE WALKED AROUND TO the gate into the courtyard and the big outdoor pool and patio. She sank into one of the deck chairs and let the darkening heat settle on her shoulders. The last time she'd been home long enough to sit by a pool was the summer of 1984. Annie had summoned Rickie home to hang out with Tom, who'd been sick with what their doctor-parents thought was encephalitis. He'd been really sick, close to death at one point. Rickie was supposedly taking a translation course and studying for graduate exams, but mostly she was painting dorm rooms with Deborah, playing tennis, and going to the bar a lot. She was relieved to go home and spend some time with her brother in the backyard suburban sanitarium.

What she recalled about that summer was the way that the chaise longue deck chairs on their suburban homestead patio took on personalities. Rickie's chair reposed with the back end of the frame raised up one click, two clicks to an oblique angle, like a hospital bed. The vinyl webbing molded itself to fit her contours. It looked like her. They'd read the *Kansas City Star*, swim in the pool, kibitz sometimes, and spend a lot of time with their eyes closed.

Tom, in the chair to her right, was skinnier than he'd been since before he hit puberty. He was twenty-five years old and had an MBA and a job in marketing for a corporation in Saint Louis. Earlier that summer, he got hit with practically paralyzing headaches. When he started seeing double, Annie flew to Saint Louis and brought Tom with her back to Shawnee Mission. He ended up spending nine days in the ICU at KU Medical Center, where Annie and CJ were professors of psychiatry. Nobody, not even the Chief of Staff, knew why or how Tom decompensated so quickly and then suddenly snapped out of the horrendous neurological crisis. When he was discharged to recuperate at home in Shawnee Mission, Annie called and asked Rickie to come home from New York and keep him company. Rickie hopped in the white Chevette the next day and headed west. When she got to the pool deck in Shawnee Mission, she and Tom didn't talk about what happened or how he was feeling, but by August, he was looking a lot less green than he had when she'd arrived a month earlier.

On most days, the chair to Rickie's left was occupied by Bill DuBois, her first and last boyfriend. He was the same color he had been for the entire twenty-six years of his life: white as a fish belly. With or without Rickie, Bill and Tom were friends. CJ and Annie had always liked Bill, and he still visited them even when Tom and Rickie were gone. He was a friend of the family, and, unlike Rickie and Tom, he was in the family business: medicine. Bill hadn't said much about his life these days, but Annie had already said that she and CJ were doing their best to keep Bill DuBois from flunking out of medical school. Bill DuBois had never flunked anything in his life, so it was clear that something was wrong with him.

As for Rickie, she was a lot more tan than she was when she drove into town from New York's Southern Tier. She was not going to be a doctor or an MBA, either. In 1984, she was a graduate student in English and was not sure exactly what she was going to be or do yet, but she had an assistantship so at least nobody had to pay tuition or dorm fees while she figured it out.

People she knew in Shawnee Mission kept telling her she was different now, that she didn't even look the same anymore. She told them it might be her haircut. Right before Annie had summoned her back to Shawnee Mission, she'd gone down to New York City with Terry Scalco, her friend/girlfriend/whatever. They went downtown to Astor Place Barbers, and Rickie got the haircut version of Calvin Klein boys' underwear for girls: tight over the ears, buzzed up the back, floppy bangs. Here in Shawnee Mission, she felt that she was a fib, a walking trick of the eye. People looked at her, with her haircut and her pink girl/boy boxers hanging out of her track shorts. First glance told them she was a boy, but a second take said she was a girl. Even though she'd grown up there and had lived most of her life in Shawnee Mission—half-way between the Shawnee Indian Mission in Fairway and the lunatic asylum at Osawatomie, she felt like a foreigner.

"Let's take that old Datsun for a spin, Rickie Lynn," Bill said as he finished his millionth cigarette. "Come on."

All month, Bill had been driving a beautifully restored white Datsun sports car, a two-seater convertible. Just after he and Rickie and Tom had first settled into their backyard deck chairs, Bill bought the car from Rickie's next-door neighbor, Dexter Bell. Rickie asked Bill why a medical student would need a sports car, but before he could answer, Tom said that doctors drove sports cars all the time. Bill was a year older than Tom and had gone to Shawnee Mission West High School and then KU. Tom thought Bill was funny and cool and sometimes acted like Bill had been his friend first.

Above them, the sky was a fine, high scrim, and they took off with the top down. Bill stopped at a liquor store and flipped Rickie a ten-dollar bill.

"You fly, I'll buy," he said.

"What do you want?" she asked him.

"Get an eight-pack of ponies and a half-pint of bourbon."

They headed south on Highway 69, all the way down to the Osawatomie exit, which would have been an hour in a regular car and was forty minutes in Bill's Datsun. He wheeled off the exit, screamed over the bridge, and took the northbound on ramp with a quick series of shifts.

"Did you ever see the Devil Worshippers out here?" Rickie asked.

"Devil Worshippers?" He looked at her and shook his head. "Do you really think there are Devil Worshippers at Osawatomie?"

"No. But Tony Burns was always saying he saw them."

"Is he the kid of that Brenda Burns?"

"Mrs. Burns? The basketball coach? Yes."

"Now there's a lunatic," Bill said. "Brenda Burns."

Rickie laughed. "I can't believe you even know her. She was my junior high basketball coach," she said. "I got drunk with her and her son Tony at the Fairyland Drive-In the summer before I went to South."

"And some other kid like Carter Pitcairn or Gary Murray, right?"

"Did you know them? Gary went to West, didn't he?"

"They both did," Bill said. "She used to have parties at her house, and one or the other of them was always getting a blow job right in the middle of everything."

"I heard about her doing that later, from somebody in my math class when I was a junior at South. But really? Really?"

"Really," he said. He looked at her and then he looked at the darkening horizon as they wheeled off the freeway at Osawatomie. "Brenda Burns is the closest thing to a Devil Worshipper you're going to see around here." He drained his last pony and chucked the empty bottle at a fence post just above the ditch. The bottle gave a tinkling pop. "Nailed it," he said. "That makes two fence posts, a mail box, and road sign for me. I win."

When they got back from the drive, Rickie was not quite ready to go to bed yet, and Bill was not quite ready to go home.

"Let's go sit by the pool and finish off this booze," he said.

Rickie nodded. Bill followed her through the house, made a quick stop in the bathroom, and sneaked out the back door to the patio. He settled into his deck chair and bathed in the moonlight. He snapped the tab on a can of beer and took the last swig of the bourbon.

Rickie watched him as she settled into her chair's sticky webbing. In the moon's bare blue glare, she felt like a hot dog on a grill, a marshmallow on a stick—about to swell up and split with all the things she was not saying to Bill or Tom or CJ or Annie or anybody else at home. Terry Scalco, the girl who sometimes called her from the Southern Tier, was not just her neighbor or just a friend. Rickie guessed she could just say to everybody, "Hey, she's my girlfriend, and I'm a lesbian," but she was not so sure how that would go over with

Annie and CJ and everybody else around there. One time, Rickie and Annie had been sitting in a new Italian restaurant in Westport, waiting for CJ to come out of the bathroom. Annie looked over at a swishy guy who squealed when the server delivered their pizza and their order of ravioli.

Annie looked at the guy and said to Rickie, "CJ would have such a hard time with a son like that."

Rickie gaped. Sometimes, Annie wore a T-shirt from what she called her feminist lady-doctor group, Women in Medicine. The logo on their T-shirts said "XX=MD." Other times, she put on strappy sandals and a sundress and showed up as a *shiksa* from a conservative family in Lincoln, Nebraska. At some point, Rickie figured she'd tell Annie and CJ she was gay. Maybe they'd say, "Oh, that's fine," or maybe they'd lock her up in Osawatomie, with Brenda Burns, the lunatics, and the Devil Worshippers.

Rickie sneaked a look at Bill DuBois. Earlier that day, she'd gotten a letter from Michael Haik. She brought the letter to her deck chair, opened it carefully, and read the letter once, twice, three times.

"What's that? A love letter?" Bill asked. His tone sounded teasing, but he was tapping a cigarette the way he did when he was annoyed.

Rickie scowled at him. "It's from my friend, Michael."

"Who's he? Some poetry fag?" He laughed and looked at Tom. Tom did not open his eyes, and Rickie told Bill to shut up.

She thought about Michael. The last time they talked on the phone, on a chilly day in May, he asked her what she thought she'd get by slaying another degree.

She frowned and pulled on the neck of the sweater Michael had given her before he'd left for New York City a few days earlier. It was big and black, with a weave as dense and heavy as chain mail. She wiped her nose on Michael's chain mail sweater. Before she could open her mouth to tell him anything, he opened his.

"I'm moving back home to Jacksonville," he said.

At that moment, she knew that whatever was wrong with him, it was serious. It had to be that bad for him to pack up, leave New York City, and move home to his parents' house in Jacksonville, Florida, where he'd grown up.

"I'll write to you," she said.

And she did. She got a letter from him in June, and though she'd written him a few more times, he hadn't written back. She was not sure what to do. Was he going to finish his dissertation, or did he leave it behind, hammered into his sweater? If so, the sweater was hers to wear now, and the dissertation was hers to write.

The last time she'd actually seen Michael, she was helping him pack up his dorm room, and Michael was talking about his mom in Jacksonville, Florida. He said that when he told his mom he was gay, his mom sent him to a shrink. When he started getting sick all the time, his mom told him that the shrink said that homosexuals were often hypochondriacs, especially with their moms. In this letter, he was telling her he still had lesions on his legs and back.

"I'm not going to Jacksonville," he had said to Rickie, then. "I'm going down to New York City for the summer, and I'm not coming back in the fall."

Rickie nodded. Michael kept saying this, but it didn't make sense. Everybody came back in the fall unless they were going abroad or graduating. He was not doing either one. Something was wrong. He kept getting rashes and diarrhea and pneumonia. Nobody was saying he had AIDS. "It's not

AIDS," everybody said, but nobody knew what was making him sick.

"I have to go to bed," she told Bill as she sat up and planted her feet on the patio. "I've got one hell of a long-ass drive back to Binghamton. When do you go back to medical school?"

"Day after tomorrow," he said. He finished off his beer. "Shit."

"Day after tomorrow? No lie? Are you ready? He shook his head. "No lie. Not at all ready." He paused, tapped out a cigarette from his pack, and laughed. "Good thing I'm so good looking."

"Good thing," she nodded. "I don't know if I'm really at all ready, either. I'm supposed to finish my master's next spring. Then what? Stay for a PhD? Jump off the Brooklyn Bridge?" She scrubbed her hair until it stood straight up.

"What's going on with you," he said. "You've been in school since you were a toddler in Montessori, and now you're sick of it? Is something wrong?"

She stared up at the blue-black sky. "No, I'm fine," she said at last. "Come on." She got up out of the deck chair, picked up the empty beer cans and the little booze bottle, and tipped her head toward the house. For a second, she thought about telling him he could spend the night if he wanted to. They could sleep on the pull-out couch in the playroom or even in the double bed in her old room upstairs. What the hell. It was not a good idea, and it was not going to happen, but even so, it was a nice thought, and she wished she could tell him.

•

BILL PULLED OUT OF the driveway, and as he drove up the street, he honked at Dexter Bell, the boy next door who was always busy fixing wrecked cars, day and night. Rickie waved to Dexter Bell, and he nodded from his driveway. Dexter Bell wasn't that smart or good looking, either, but he could fix cars. That night, he'd turned on the front lights and the garage lights and was working on an MG Midget.

"Nice car," Rickie said to Dexter Bell as she walked across the yard.

"This is nothing. You want it?"

"I like the color."

"Stoplight green."

"Stoplight red?"

"What's the color that says go? OK. How much?"

"Five hundred bucks."

She paused for a second. She figured she could withdraw the cash from her savings account, buy the car from Dexter Bell, and head out West. Then she shook her head, waved at him, and went inside. The next day, she left for New York in the white Chevette.

Rickie sat up in the deck chair outside CJ's apartment. She hadn't thought about Dexter Bell's MG in years, but now she was wondering if she'd made a mistake, if the MG could have taken her out to some wide-open land she'd never even thought of before. Now, there she was, again: to the north was the Shawnee Indian Mission; to the south was Osawatomie, keeping an eye on the kids driving around chucking beer bottles at road signs, on the parents driving to or from work, on everybody who'd been displaced, forgotten, or stuck in this place that wasn't a city or a town or a farm or state forest or a reservation, not a Pale of Settlement or a kibbutz or a ghetto or a concentration camp, maybe a little bit like a *shtetl*. It didn't feel like home, this place, but at least it was still familiar.

She left the patio, now sinking from a lavender glaze to a dark purple tarp, and went back to CJ's apartment. In the living room was Annie's old leather chair, and Rickie sat down in it. She was pretty sure that if Annie were alive, she'd say that she understood how she and Tom might think that somebody in CJ's condition would want to die and would not want any special measures. She'd tell Rickie that CJ had made his choice; he wanted to live. She'd advise her to gather together, huddle up, gird her loins. CJ did not want to die, and he did want all possible measures taken. He was not ready for death, which was more powerful than psychiatry and other kinds of medicine. He must have known what he was talking about, having by that time watched death come for his sister, his mother, his wife, his brothers. When Rickie thought about death coming, she imagined destructive insects like termites or carpenter ants systematically devouring the house plank by plank, beam by beam until nothing was left but a pile of sawdust.

7

THE NEXT MORNING, RICKIE opened the apartment door to grab the morning paper, and there in the hall was CJ's neighbor, Mrs. Levine.

"Let's walk over to Cosentino's," Mrs. Levine said. "And have a cup of coffee."

The buffalo head at Cosentino's watched them get their coffee and sit down. Mrs. Levine wanted to know how CJ was doing.

"It's terrible," she said when Rickie gave her a brief update. "Have you been in touch with your relatives? The *mischpocheh* need to know."

Rickie blinked. She knew that *mischpocheh* meant the extended family, but she didn't know how far that family extended in Mrs. Levine's definition. "Um," she began. "Well, my brother Tom is in New Zealand, but I've talked to him."

Mrs. Levine nodded and reached out to pat Rickie's hand. "Relatives? Cousins? Call your cousins. Families need to know who is where and what's going on in an emergency." She straightened her arm. "I survived the Holocaust, you know," she said. "I don't have a tattoo on my forearm, and the only reason is that my grandfather got our family out of Germany in 1939. My grandparents, my parents, my siblings plus two uncles, three aunts, and cousins. We got on a ship in Bremerhaven and got off at Ellis Island."

Rickie nodded. "Same with my grandmother."

Mrs. Levine nodded. "Some of the *mischpocheh* went to Chicago and Saint Louis. The rest stayed in New York and

57

are still there." She paused. "Well, Bobby was there. Now they're all gone."

Rickie reached for the coffee carafe and refilled their coffee cups. Mrs. Levine's son Bobby had died of AIDS in 1990, just before the arrival of the clinical cocktails. "I have one uncle left in New York," she said to Mrs. Levine. "In Rochester."

Mrs. Levine patted her hand again. Rickie put her hand on top of Mrs. Levine's. Usually, Rickie Lynn Jackson was not the type of person to hold hands with old people she barely knew, but Mrs. Levine had said many times that Annie and CJ had been a great comfort to her when her son Bobby was sick, especially Annie. Rickie always figured that Annie was better at dealing with AIDS when it involved people who weren't her daughter.

"I am so sorry about Bobby," Rickie said. She'd met Bobby once or twice when they'd both been home for holiday visits. They weren't exactly friends, but they were friendly. "One of my best friends died in 1985. It was horrible."

"I hope he wasn't alone," Mrs. Levine said.

Rickie hadn't cried about Michael Haik in a long time, but suddenly she felt tears start in her eyes. "He wasn't alone," she said in a quaking voice. "His brother was with him. He wrote to me later and told me that Michael's last words were 'Keep calm.'"

Mrs. Levine smiled and put her hand on top of the pile on the table. "What a catastrophe," she said and pulled her hands back so she could pick up her coffee cup. She took a sip and eyed Rickie. "Tell your family," she said again. "People need to know."

•

THE BUFFALO ON THE wall in Cosentino's watched as Rickie

and Mrs. Levine left the store. They walked back to the apartment building and took the elevator to their floor. One more time before she went into her apartment, Mrs. Levine said to Rickie, "Call the *mischpocheh*."

Rickie nodded and said good-bye before she went into CJ's apartment and shut the door. She went to the kitchen, consulted CJ's address book by the phone, and called her cousin, Becky Jackson.

Before Becky's dad, Uncle Marty, had died two years earlier, Rickie didn't call Becky very often, even though Becky and her sister Esti and Rickie and Rickie's brother Tom had been close as kids. Now Tom and Becky both lived in Saint Louis and saw each other frequently. From Tom, Rickie got the news about Becky and her partner, Sue Wilson, and their son, Charles Martin Wilson Jackson—named after CJ and Marty. A nice little Jewish boy more perfect than Charlie they could not have ordered or built from a kit. After Annie and Uncle Marty died and then Uncle Kenny, the middle brother, died, Rickie started calling Becky for more regular check-ins, more frequent family talk.

Becky picked up the call on the first ring. "Rickie," she said. "I'm so glad you called. Did you hear about Uncle Jimmy?"

"Uncle Jimmy? In Rochester? What's wrong with Uncle Jimmy?"

"*Oi vey*. You know he had that aneurysm?"

"Oh, yes. I heard about that. Just before Christmas, right? CJ was worried about him."

"Well, then he got pneumonia," Becky said. She stopped and blew her nose. "He died yesterday."

Rickie felt as if a winter wind had barreled in. "What? Yesterday? I am sorry. That is horrible. I had no idea. How did you hear about all of this?"

"My sister Esti is in touch with our cousin, Timothy Jackson," Becky said. "Timothy called her this morning, and Esti called me. I know Tom's away, but I left a message at his office and was just about to call you. I figured you'd be in Kansas City with CJ."

She was talking about the *mischpocheh*: Esti, her sister, and their cousin, Timothy, who was Uncle Jimmy's only child. Tom and Rickie had never met Timothy. Esti and Becky they knew, and they saw them and Uncle Marty and Aunt Frances often when the kids were little and a lot when Marty was at the Menninger Clinic in Topeka for a few years in the late 70s. A few times in the early 80s, they met Uncle Kenny when he came for a holiday or a long weekend, but they never once met Uncle Jimmy or his wife, Donna, or Timothy, their son. Now Uncle Jimmy was dead.

"I never ever even met Uncle Jimmy," Rickie said to Becky. "Or Donna or Timothy, for that matter."

"The brothers had their stuff," Becky said.

"Yes," Rickie said. "It's Jewish *meshugaas*. But several of the Jews and spouses in this *meshugaas* are psychiatrists. You'd think they'd know how to manage it."

"Your mom, my mom, my dad," Becky counted.

"That's what I'm saying," Rickie said. "I mean, out of all of them, surely you'd think that Annie would have made everybody deal with their aggressions with each other and then sit down to a big dinner. Or that Aunt Frances or Uncle Marty would have lined up couches for a great big giant psychoanalysis. But no."

"I know," Becky said. "Don't you think all this *meshugaas* comes from their dead sister?"

Rickie gulped. "Yes, Eileen," she said. "Good point."

Eileen Jackson, Sol and Leah Jackson's only daughter and

everybody's favorite, was diagnosed with osteosarcoma at age nineteen. She was dead before she was twenty-two. The specter of Eileen's sickness and death hung over every encounter and every conversation, but nobody ever really talked about her horrible sickness and death. Even CJ, who loved to discourse at length about everything, didn't say much about Eileen. What Rickie knew from the most detailed conversation she and Tom had had with CJ was that when Eileen was diagnosed with cancer, the doctors wanted to amputate her leg. Eileen said no, and she died not long after.

"It was her only chance," CJ said. "But she wouldn't do it."

"I wouldn't want some doctor chopping off my leg, either," Rickie said.

"But they didn't have the medicines then that they do now. Amputation was the best way to remove the cancer," CJ explained.

"What happened when she said no?" Tom asked.

"Why didn't your mom make her get her leg chopped off?" Rickie asked. "If I had cancer in my leg, I bet I would have yelled my head off about not wanting an amputation, but Mom would have made me do it anyway."

"She kept her leg, and the cancer spread," CJ said. "She got sicker, and she died. She was twenty-one years old."

"How old were you?" Rickie asked.

"I was nineteen and in college," CJ said. "I almost flunked out of the University of Rochester. My mother was up all night, crying and screaming, all the time."

Tom and Rickie shuddered, and that was as far as the conversation went. Esti and Becky didn't know any more about Eileen than they did.

"So Eileen's dead and then Uncle Kenny and then your dad and now Uncle Jimmy?" Rickie said at last.

"Uncle CJ is the last of the five," Becky said. "Give him my love, and please tell him to take good care of himself."

After she finished the call with Becky, Rickie called Deborah Walker. Her call went to Deborah's answering machine, and Rickie didn't bother even saying hello. "The Cossacks are galloping," she said. "Call me."

She hung up the phone and sat down by the kitchen window in CJ's apartment: a southern view of a high sky and a wide horizon. She figured she'd be able to tell Mrs. Levine later that she'd called the *mischpocheh*, which, in Rickie's mind, included Deborah Walker.

In the dorm at Binghamton early in the fall semester of Rickie's freshman year, she and Deborah had done a little Jewish geography and found that their Jewish relatives came from the same places, more or less. Deborah's grandmother on her mom's side was a Litvak, and her grandfather's family was from Poland and the Ukraine, same as Rickie's grandparents on CJ's side.

CJ's dad, Sol Jackson, was born in Dnepropetrovsk, and the family left for Argentina when he was a toddler. He came to the United States from Buenos Aires when he was a teenager, just in time to get drafted for World War I. After the war, he turned up in Topeka, Kansas, where he met Leah, who'd recently arrived from Poland.

Rickie thought Jackson was probably a mispronunciation or some immigration officer's invention. Then her cousin Esti found some papers in Uncle Marty's files, and one document listed Sol's name as Salomon Javitsky.

"My cousin said that Sol, my grandfather, was the one to change his name. Maybe he didn't want an ethnic-sounding name when he got through immigration, so he changed it to Jackson," Rickie said to Deborah.

"*Goyische*," Deborah Walker said. "At least he didn't change it from Javitsky to Jones. How did your parents meet?"

"They met in medical school at the University of Nebraska," Rickie said. "On my mom's side, the relatives came to Nebraska from Bavaria."

"First folks to support Hitler," Deborah Walker observed.

"Who knows about those Nebraska Bavarians?" Rickie said. "I don't know if they thought CJ was some horrible Jewish monster, or if they just figured that Annie was completely unpredictable, anyway, going off to college and then medical school. A Jew? Why not?"

"Did CJ ever say anything about them?"

"Nothing negative, other than sometimes calling them 'the Krauts,'" she said. "He liked them, I think. We'd go up there for holidays sometimes and have their bone-in glazed hams and their homemade sausages and their potato salad made with Miracle Whip and their date cookies that tasted like *hamantaschen* but were not. He'd eat every bite."

"What about holidays at your house?"

"The farm relatives sometimes came at Easter," Rickie said. "Ham, scalloped potatoes, peas, dinner rolls, apple pie and cinnamon ice cream. Whole milk. Yum."

Deborah Walker was lactose intolerant and allergic to pollen. Miracle Whip she found intolerable as well. She wouldn't have lasted five minutes on that farm, or at any of the *goyische* holidays that the Jacksons celebrated. She clicked her tongue. "And Passover?"

"We had that, too," Rickie said. "Matzoh ball soup, chopped liver, brisket, roasted potatoes, that apple stuff. Charoses? Halitoses?"

"Charoset."

"Yes, that. We wore baseball caps for yarmulkes and had a

seder. Annie had a Passover plate and the whole bit. Matzohs, herb-dunking, reading the Haggadah. Tom and I called it the Haganah."

"I wonder what that is all about," Deborah Walker mused. "A Jew marries a *shiksa* who becomes a Jew, culturally."

"Did your dad become a cultural Jew?"

"My dad's black," Deborah said flatly. "My mom is still pretty Jewish but is also culturally black. She and my dad have this collection of Jim Crow memorabilia. Colored Only signs and stuff. Never forget."

"Assimilation," Rickie said. "Mix in. Or maybe more like keep your friends close and your enemies closer."

"Closer. Sure. Why not?" Deborah said. "Sit down and eat with them. Take them to bed. Next thing you know, they're your relatives."

•

As she finished her message to Deborah Walker's answering machine, the call waiting beeped. Rickie switched lines, and the ICU nurse told Rickie that since CJ was holding his own off the ventilator, the plan was to move him to the regular Cardiac Unit later that day. It sounded like progress. Rickie thanked the nurse and decided to bring CJ some of his own clothes.

She went into CJ's walk-in closet and opened up his armoire. The cubby-like shelves were stuffed with T-shirts, shorts, and sweatpants in various colors and textures. She extracted a couple of CJ's New York Knicks T-shirts, two pair of elastic-waist shorts, and a well-worn sweatshirt from Washington University, Tom's alma mater.

In one of the two armoire drawers were enough pairs of white socks for a lifetime, and in the one below it was an equally huge number of knit boxer shorts. She grabbed six pairs of boxers and six pairs of socks and set them on the floor of the closet. She glanced around for some kind of suitcase or tote bag and saw that somebody had been in the closet with a box of plastic garbage bags. Tom had said that he was going to weed through CJ's clothes and *vorf* things that he hadn't worn in years and wasn't likely to wear ever again. Apparently, he hadn't gotten far because the clothes were all still on hangers, folded in stacks on the closet shelves, and stuffed into the armoire. The garbage bags were still nestled in their easy-access box.

She thought about extracting a plastic garbage bag and stuffing it with CJ's T-shirts, shorts, socks, and boxers, but she didn't reach for the box of bags. To her, it seemed wrong to show up at KU Medical Center, where CJ and Annie had been distinguished professors for many years, with CJ's clothes packed in a garbage bag. Somebody might get the idea that she thought CJ's stuff was garbage or that CJ himself was garbage, or that KU Med Center was a dumpster and CJ was now just a new part of the garbage in it, and Rickie was just adding to the trash pile with the plastic bag of his clothes.

"A tote bag or a duffel bag," she muttered aloud in the closet. "That'll work."

She glanced up at the shelves above the clothes rack and saw sweatshirts and pants, tracksuits, and sweaters that CJ had not worn in years. In a corner, she spotted empty laundry baskets nestled together. "Why have one when you can have three?" she said.

She grabbed the pile of clothes from the closet floor and went out to the living room. In the hall closet, way on the end on a chest-level pantry shelf, she found the stash of tote bags. She extracted one from a psychiatric convention in 1987, sat down on the couch and opened it wide. In the bottom was a snapshot of Rickie, Annie, and CJ in front of an inn in the Lake District in England. The conference had been in Birmingham that year, and Annie had invited Rickie to come with her and CJ to spend a few days in London, drive up to Birmingham and spend a few days with her doctor-friend in Birmingham. Then, after the conference, she'd planned a side trip to the Lake District, mostly for Rickie, the English major. In the photo, everybody was smiling, and they all looked happy.

She began packing the socks in the bottom of the bag, and suddenly she felt like bawling. Since Annie had died, CJ had made one or two trips to Mexico, and that was it: no conferences, no tote bags. And now he was a patient in the hospital where he used to be a distinguished professor, and it seemed like the chances of him getting well enough to come back to his apartment were getting slimmer by the day. He'd left his home in the morning, expecting to be back just past lunchtime from the angiogram he didn't want in the first place. Now he was still gone, and Rickie was looking through CJ's stuff as if he were not ever coming back. In that moment, his tidy living room looked like a hazardous waste site, a landfill, a dump.

•

SHE LEFT THE BLAZER in the visitor lot at KU Medical Center and saw on the sign near the information desk when she walked in that in ten minutes, there was an AA meeting in the rehab unit on the fifth floor of the old hospital wing, just below the locked psych ward. The sign seemed meant for her, or at least it seemed like a good idea to go to a meeting before she went to the cardiac unit to take stock of what had to be a complicated mess with CJ. She started walking without even thinking, climbing stairs, just following her feet that knew the way around this part of the hospital from having been born here, visiting here with her doctor-parents and their friends as a kid, and working here as a teenager.

When Tom turned sixteen and reached the Age of Work, Annie arranged for him to get a part-time job at KU Medical Center. He started out as a messenger in the pharmacy. Two years later, he found himself a better job as an orderly in the OR. He fixed it so that when Rickie turned sixteen, she got his old job as a pharmacy messenger.

The job was simple. Nurses and doctors would send prescriptions through the pneumatic tube system that snaked through the hospital. The pharmacists would fill the orders and then Rickie would sit at the messenger desk—an area in the pharmacy basement where, aside from occasionally putting stickers on bottles of methadone for the free clinics, she could do homework or read in between her rounds. When the prescriptions were ready, she'd go upstairs, load them into a double-decker cart on wheels, and make the deliveries.

Usually, a delivery round took her half an hour or forty-five minutes or so, unless she had to deliver to the sixth-floor locked ward. Then she'd have to take the elevator all the way up there, ring a bell, wait for somebody to buzz her in, maneuver the cart into the door, unload the stuff as fast as she could at the nurse's station which was right inside the door, and get the hell out of there before the door slammed shut. Tom told her never to say anything to anybody about the stuff she was delivering, especially to the sixth floor, but she did wonder how it could be that a doctor in a hospital could order a six-pack of beer for a patient by sending a written, signed prescription to the pharmacy, with the expectation that order would be filled not by a bartender and a cocktail waitress but by a fully trained, licensed pharmacist and delivered by a high school girljock wearing a white jacket that looked like a cross between a busboy uniform and a junior-grade medical coat.

The pharmacy that took drink orders from the locked ward at KU Medical Center served Falstaff beer. The commercials for Falstaff playing on TV and the radio featured a jingle whose main line was "We make beer for guys who like it." Some of the guys who liked it were in locked psych wards at KUMC. Some of the guys who liked beer, Falstaff or not, were girls in white jackets who played softball and went to a big suburban high school.

"Falstaff," she said out loud as she made her way to the rehab unit on the fifth floor. She could just see the cans: cream-colored with a yellow and brown shield. The shield, boasting the beer name in red letters, suggested some kind of coat of arms— maybe meant to confer royalty upon the drinker, as if Falstaff were a famous king of jolly old England and not a vain, rowdy bloke, full of hot air. Kids in Shawnee Mission tried to get their underage hands on Miller or Coors or Olympia beer. Dads who spent a lot of time in their garages drank Falstaff: those dads and the inmates in the locked ward.

She pulled open the door marked *5* and took a second to orient herself on the fifth floor. Across the hall and down, a door to what looked like a conference room was open wide, and she could hear people talking. She made for the open door and saw somebody placing big placards featuring the Twelve Steps on a big easel at the end of the long conference table. The talk ceased when she paused the doorway, but that always happened when a new person walked into a meeting.

"Hi," she said. "I'm Rickie."

A chorus replied, "Hi, Rickie," and she knew she was in the right place.

8

THE MEETING'S TOPIC WAS the First Step, and people around the table were talking about the various ways that their powerlessness over alcohol and catastrophes in their unmanageable lives led them to AA. Rickie introduced herself and said that her alcohol autobiography began with the first can of Olympia she popped in the back seat of her basketball coach's Fiat, headed for the Fairyland Drive-In in Kansas City. The beginning of her story in AA, she said, began in Minneapolis not long after Michael Haik's death.

"I always found it hard to pinpoint the beginnings and ends of catastrophes, aftermaths, recoveries, but I can determine a turning point in Binghamton, New York, on the day after Michael Haik died, May 10, 1985, right after I had turned in my thesis and finished up my master's degree," she told the group.

People around the room nodded and thanked her for sharing. She sat back and thought about that day. The Director of Graduate Studies had called Rickie in her dorm room to tell her that her friend Michael Haik had died at his parents' house in Florida. She stood there with the phone in her hand in utter, shocked silence. The Director of Graduate Studies waited an extra long beat and then said, "I understand that this is horrible news for you, and I am sorry to be its bearer. Please let me know if I can help at all. Come by my office and we can talk if you want."

Rickie said, "Thanks," which was all she could manage, and then she hung up the phone and sat down on the edge of her narrow dorm room bed, stunned. Earlier that semester, she had decided, sort of, that she wasn't coming back in the fall to work on a PhD. She' d planned to stay on campus until the dorms closed at the end of May. In case she changed her mind, which she figured she'd probably do, she'd go into the DGS's office, explain why she had to get her assistantship extended, and then go down to New York City and hang out with Michael Haik or go out to Long Island and shack up with her on-again, off-again girlfriend, Terry Scalco, or maybe just go home for the summer. Or something.

For a second on that dark day in May in Binghamton, she considered running over to the English department office and seeing if she could come back in the fall to work on a PhD. The DGS was a nice guy and would understand her ambivalence. In her head, she rattled off a list of possible courses of study: pretense in the short stories of Katherine Mansfield, or portraiture in Bloomsbury if she wanted to go the Brit Lit route, or the gay subtext in the novels of Willa Cather if she decided to gamble on her family roots in Nebraska and do American Lit. Then, after the phone rang again and then one more time with grad school friends wanting to know if the rumors about Michael were true, Rickie decided that the thing to do was to leave town.

By that time, Deborah had already left. Most of her other friends were in their off-campus apartments on the West Side, and she was pretty much alone in the graduate student dorm. On campus, there was a full-service pub in the basement of the student union, a cheap cafeteria on the first floor, and a food coop on the second floor. There was a post office near the library and laundry in her dorm, so it was easy enough to manage the tasks of daily life without leaving campus, unless the task was to get drunk in a dorm room. In that case, a person needed to make a quick trip to a nearby grocery store and pick up a six-pack in the beer cooler aisle. Still stunned and moving like a steer in the stockyards, she made her way to the Chevette and drove down Vestal Parkway to Grand Union, the closest grocery store with a beer aisle.

Grand Union was lit up like a carnival midway, and the beer brands were barking: Genesee Light in royal blue cans, Schaefer in brown bottles with pry-off caps; Rolling Rock in stoplight green cans; Carling Black Label in white cans, cheap. The beer aisle at Grand Union was so much better than anyplace like it in Kansas, where all they sold was weak, watery 3.2 percent piss-beer–just barely better than nothing.

She picked up a six-pack of Genny Light, a box of cereal, a quart of milk, a pack of thin-sliced turkey, and the smallest loaf of bread she could find. She lugged her shopping bag to her dorm room and stuffed her goods into the tiny refrigerator. Then she tuned in WHRW, the campus radio station, cracked the first beer, and listened to the club music that the dj was playing on a show called "Heritage."

The rooms in her dorm were meant to be doubles, but most of the grad students wanted singles. Each room, no matter the number of occupants had two twin beds, two desks with chairs, two dressers, two closets. Some grad students just left the arrangement, as if their roommate were an invisible friend. Others piled the second mattress on one of the bed frames, disassembled the extra frame and stowed it underneath the bed or in one of the closets. The two desks were somewhat useful as they were: one for a typewriter and the other for the rest of the work.

In Rickie's room, set up for an invisible roommate friend, the empty beer cans stood in formation on the window ledge, watching. She drank and packed half the night and most of the next day, stopping only to eat a bowl of cereal or run down the hall to pee and grab a drink of water.

After a quick return trip to Grand Union for another six-pack, she called to say good-bye to Terry Scalco, her girl-friend who wasn't quite an ex yet but was already a memory. Her phone rang a couple more times after she finished with Terry, but she didn't answer it. She left the beer cans out by the dumpster for some lucky person to find and return to Grand Union for the five-cent deposit, and then she made a bag of sandwiches for the road, packed up the stereo, and spent the remaining hours of her last night in a sleeping bag on top of one of the stripped single beds. The next morning, she checked out of her dead-empty dorm and left town.

She drove all the way home to Shawnee Mission in one long day. Downstairs in the playroom, where Annie knew Rickie liked to sleep when she felt out of sorts, a card waited for her on the coffee table in front of the couch. Neither one of her parents were big on social niceties like condolence cards, and she figured that Annie must have sent CJ on a special trip to the drug store to get one. On the outside of the card was a drawing of roses, looking a little bit like the roses that Annie and CJ had planted around the pool in the back yard. Inside, in silver ink script, the message said, "We are sorry for your loss." Each of them had signed the card, not just Annie signing for both of them. It seemed weird and oddly formal, and beyond that, Rickie couldn't even yet fathom the edges of her loss. She felt it like a slowly spreading flood, the way that Indian Creek, across the street, topped its banks and snuck quietly into the neighbors' basements after storms. Even so, the cards made her feel a little better or at least a little less bewildered, bereft, besieged, beleaguered, fraught, careworn, exhausted, and pissed off.

Two days after she read her condolence card late at night in Shawnee Mission, she called Deborah Walker. Deborah had moved out of her dorm room a week earlier than Rickie, and she'd just moved into the duplex she'd bought in Minneapolis. Her girlfriend, a rugby player named Cricket, had moved in with her.

Deborah said to Rickie, "Why don't you come up here until you figure out what you want to do? We'll keep an eye on you. The hooker who is living in the upstairs unit needs a roommate. You can have the extra room if you want it."

"The hooker?" Rickie said. "From the rugby team?"

Deborah laughed. "No, the other kind of hooker."

"What?" Rickie said. She couldn't tell if Deborah was teasing. "Does she work out of your house?"

"Rickie Ricardo," Deborah said in her "calm down" voice. "She's retired. She got in some trouble with drugs and prostitution, and she asked Cricket for some help. Her name is Tracy Chick. She was Cricket's first girlfriend. She moved in, and we all want somebody else in that unit paying rent."

"Tracy Chick?" Rickie repeated. "Is that for real?"

"Her last name's a mile long," Deborah said. "Everybody calls her Tracy Chick."

At the end of the not very long conversation, Rickie was not only set to move into the vacant room in Deborah's duplex, but she could also go to work at the grocery store where Deborah's brother was a manager until she figured out what she was going to do next. Rickie wasn't exactly sure how she was going to explain to CJ and Annie that she was going to work at a grocery store and live in a duplex in Minneapolis with Deborah, her rugby dyke girlfriend, and Tracy Chick, the hooker, but she figured they wouldn't protest too much or even ask for details if she said straight off that she had a place to live and a job. Eventually, she was planning to return to graduate school, somewhere, for a PhD, which was actually OK with them, though they didn't exactly know about the eventually part. They all knew that Rickie wouldn't last very long in the playroom at the house in Shawnee Mission. She told them her plan at dinner.

Annie said, "You don't play rugby. How do you know these women rugby players in Minneapolis?"

"Deborah Walker," Rickie said. She paused and tried to think of something else to add. "Their house is close to the U of M, in case I go there for a PhD, and I can work for Deborah's brother in the meantime."

CJ said, "It takes leather balls to play rugby."

That was the end of the conversation. Rickie left two days later.

It didn't take her long to settle in her room on the top floor of the Park Avenue duplex. On a late June evening, Rickie was drinking a can of Blatz Light, the cheapest beer at the nearby liquor store, and watching a tiny black-and-white TV. Martina and Chrissie were playing tennis at Wimbledon when in walked Tracy Chick. She sat down next to Rickie on her futon, which was folded against the wall like a couch with no legs.

"Who do you like better," Tracy Chick asked. "Sylvia Plath or Anne Sexton?"

Tracy Chick was practically touching Rickie, and she'd never done that before. Rickie was thinking that futon rolled into a legless couch on the floor can be pretty comfortable once you flop down on it, but it's not that easy to get up once you are down there.

"Did Deborah tell you to ask me that?" she said at last.

Tracy Chick shook her honey-colored ponytail. "No. Deborah likes Judy Grahn, of course. I'm asking you."

Rickie tried not to squirm on the futon. A person wouldn't really pick out Tracy Chick for a hooker with that ponytail and the leotard thing she wore all the time like a Mormon temple undergarment, but she didn't really look straight, either.

"When I was an English major undergraduate," Rickie began. "It seemed that everybody was crazy about Plath." Rickie paused. Sometimes it was OK to talk poetry with people she didn't know very well, and other times, it was just a big huge embarrassment, usually ending with the person who started the conversation about poetry trying to get out of it by insulting the English major person who actually knew a thing or two. She did like Sylvia Plath, but a lot of people she knew at Binghamton thought that Anne Sexton was actually cooler. Finally, Rickie said, "I like Plath's bee poems."

"Which one's your favorite?"

"Um," Rickie said. "The 'her lion-red body, her wings of glass' bee poem. 'Stings.'"

Tracy Chick gripped Rickie's forearm. "I love that poem," she said. She let go of Rickie's arm, pushed down on the futon, and practically launched herself out the door and across the hall into her room. Rickie heard her rummaging around and saying, "Where is it?"

Rickie called across the hall. "I've got a copy of *Ariel* if that's what you are looking for."

"You do?" she said as she reappeared in the doorway. "Really?"

"Yes. When I was a junior in college, I bought this book on a study-abroad trip to England."

Before Rickie could even finish telling her that she'd visited the house where Plath had gassed herself, Tracy Chick came in and sat down next to her again. While Martina and Chrissie played their match on the little TV, Tracy Chick read aloud from her favorite Plath poems in Rickie's book. Then she went across the hall again and came back with a book of poems by Anne Sexton.

Tracy Chick's well-thumbed book opened itself on her lap. "This is my favorite," she said. "'A woman like that is not a woman, quite/ I have been her kind.'"

Rickie nodded. It seemed best to say nothing.

Tracy Chick gave her a long look. Then she got up and went across the hall to her room again and shut the door. Rickie just sat there, half aware of the ball-thwacking on the little TV, half-hoping that Tracy Chick would return in nothing but hooker underwear.

Back came Tracy Chick with a mirror, a baggie, and a piece of plastic straw, and a razor blade. She walked over to Rickie's desk, sat down in the chair, pushed the typewriter off to one side, and put the mirror in its place. Then she set up some lines on the mirror, turned to Rickie, and held out the little piece of straw.

"Want some?" She smiled, and Rickie noticed that Tracy Chick's teeth were small and slightly gray.

Rickie moved toward the desk, and then she stopped. She and Deborah drank beer and sometimes tequila; Cricket smoked a lot of pot, and Tracy Chick, she knew, had been or was an IV drug user. Cricket had told her that Tracy had made a lot of money as a prostitute and had gotten herself into a big heap of trouble shooting coke. She showed up on the doorstep of Deborah Walker's duplex looking for help.

"Coke?" Rickie asked.

"No," Tracy Chick said. She fussed with the lines on the mirror. "I stopped using coke when I quit working at the brothel," she said. "I got in too much trouble."

"The brothel?" Rickie exclaimed. She imagined swinging

lamps and red curtains, a secret password at the door, a shop-worn madam. "Really?"

Tracy Chick gave a rueful laugh. "Technically, a hotel. But really a brothel," she said. "A whorehouse."

Rickie squirmed on the futon. A whorehouse sounded like something from a logging camp in the Wild West or maybe Belle Watling's second-floor digs in *Gone With the Wind*. She couldn't tell if Tracy Chick was teasing. "So what is that if it isn't coke?" she asked and pointed at the mirror.

"Crank," Tracy Chick said.

"Crank?"

"You've never heard of crank?" Tracy said and shook her head. "I thought you just came back from New York."

"I was upstate," Rickie said. "People did coke."

Tracy Chick laughed and tipped her ponytail at Rickie. "Give this a try," she said. "I bet you'll like it."

"All right," she said. She wasn't at all sure that she'd like it or that she even wanted to try it, but she didn't quite know how to say no, either. Rickie pushed herself off the futon and took the piece of straw from Tracy Chick. The crank smelled like some kind of industrial cleaning material. She rubbed her burning nose and put the straw down. "Do you think Deborah will kill me if I drink the last beer?"

"Probably," said Tracy Chick.

She returned to the futon with the last beer, and Tracy Chick sniffed up those lines and started talking. She said she'd come down from Cloquet, Minnesota, up on the Iron Range, and had gone to the University of Minnesota for a while. She was studying poetry and women writers, but she got mixed up with some big time drug users and dropped out.

"What happened?"

"I'd met Cricket by then," Tracy Chick continued. "You

know she was my first girlfriend, right? Anyway, Cricket took me to St. Jude's for a chemical dependency evaluation, just to see if I maybe had a problem." She stopped and rubbed her nose. "I ended up checking in right on the spot. I didn't even go home to collect a notebook, a toothbrush, a change of clothes."

"Really?" Rickie said. "What did you wear while you were there?" She was trying to envision Tracy Chick with her ass peeking out the crack of a hospital gown.

"Cricket brought me some clothes," she said. "I stayed for thirty days. After that, I went to a halfway house where I decided I was going to be a chemical dependency counselor."

"Really?"

Tracy Chick looked at Rickie and then at the TV. "Really. I was going to write poetry and work as a drug counselor, but instead, Cricket and I broke up, and I had a terrific relapse instead and went back to IV drugs and sex work." She paused and looked at Rickie, who was hoping that Tracy Chick would lean over and kiss her. She went back to her story. "And now I'm a junkie whore," said Tracy Chick.

The tennis match ended, and the little TV filled the room with a blue-gray murk. The futon seemed to unroll itself. The pillows and the ancient sleeping bag, so well worn that it was a perfect summer blanket, rose up like charmed snakes out of the wicker basket in the corner and arranged themselves on the futon.

The TV watched as Tracy Chick and Rickie got under the covers. She felt Tracy Chick scooch in behind her, run her hand across Rickie's back and then down and around to rest right below her solar plexus. She rested her chin on Rickie's shoulder and said, "Shhh."

•

Tracy Chick started sleeping with Rickie in her futon whenever she was home at night and felt like sleeping, which was not that often. They started having sex in Rickie's room whenever they were both home and wide awake in the morning, which was often enough during that summer, especially after Rickie got a snootful of Tracy Chick's crank.

Rickie was completely taken up and in by the experience of having sex with a stone cold professional who was not on call, not at work. She wasn't faking it or pretending. Or so Rickie thought. Tracy Chick would shoot crank for days on end, and then she'd take a Nembutal and crash for sixteen hours straight. Rickie was trying to balance the Blatz Light with the crank Tracy would line up for her with the nighttime hours at Deborah's brother's grocery store. Deborah thought the whole thing was crazy, but to Rickie, it didn't matter. It occurred to her that Tracy Chick was just having sex with her to taunt Cricket and that Rickie was a distraction, a midmorning snack. That didn't matter, either. Tracy Chick was an IV drug user, and there was talk about IV drug users and AIDS, but Tracy Chick, Rickie told herself, was not a gay man and neither was she. The danger didn't matter that much to Rickie, and neither did Deborah's warnings and admonishments: not enough to quit or stop.

By the end of August, Tracy Chick wasn't paying her rent. She stopped sleeping in Rickie's futon, and then her car got repossessed. Then things started disappearing around the house: Rickie's Walkman, Deborah's power drill, a jar of change that Cricket stored in a kitchen cabinet. At the end of the long Labor Day weekend, Cricket, Deborah, and Rickie returned to the duplex from a trip up north to Deborah's parents' cabin. Tracy Chick was gone.

Not long after Tracy Chick disappeared from Park Avenue,

Rickie and Deborah went to a fundraiser party for Cricket's rugby team at Foxy's, the lesbian bar across the river in Saint Paul. Deborah introduced Rickie to her friend Diane, a PE teacher at the downtown community college. When Diane heard that Rickie had worked in the writing center and taught composition at Binghamton, she told her she'd heard that the dean was looking for composition instructors.

"The dean's name is Lillian Campbell," Diane said. "Call her tomorrow. Tell her that I told you to call. The quarter starts next week."

Rickie nodded, and the next day, she called Lillian Campbell, who asked her if she could come in that afternoon for an interview. Rickie didn't feel prepared, really, but she figured that for the first time since May, she was not drunk, not high on crank, and not hungover, so she might as well give it a shot. Deborah looked through Rickie's closet for a decent outfit while Rickie dug around for her transcripts and a resume. While Rickie took a shower and washed her hair, Deborah ironed Rickie's shirt and pants. Then, since Rickie's car had been totaled by that drunk bastard and her parents had decided that if Rickie wanted another car, she could buy it herself, Deborah and Rickie caught a bus downtown to the community college. While Rickie met with Lillian Campbell and the English department chair, Deborah and Diane shot baskets in the gym. When the interview was finished, Rickie had a schedule of classes for the just-about-to-start fall quarter.

The next day, Rickie returned to the community college campus to sign papers, get copies of the course texts from the bookstore, and pick up keys to her office. The English department had a suite in the Fine Arts building, but the office space for new hires was pretty much the same kind of situation she'd had in graduate school: a desk and a file cabinet in a big room full of other desks and file cabinets occupied by other part-time instructors. It wasn't great, but it wasn't grad school, and it wasn't night stock in Deborah's brother's grocery store. Rickie put her books and a few pencils on her desk and felt the tiniest little turn in her fortunes.

Not long after classes started, Rickie was chatting in the break room with a guy named Bob Larson who taught Human Services courses and worked the desk in the student health clinic.

"Some of them need help with the usual depression and anxiety," Bob Larson was saying. "But I'm finding that a lot of people are struggling with chemical dependency. Alcohol. Drugs, you know how it goes."

Rickie felt her eyes widen. Her nose itched. She had a headache from the cheap beer she'd drunk the night before at Foxy's. "What do you do for them?"

Bob Larson looked at her for a long moment and then continued. "Mostly, we just talk. I can make referrals, but sometimes it's good just to talk and put things in perspective." He paused and eyed Rickie again. "Come on. I'll show you what I do."

It seemed like some kind of line or a trap, and Rickie could easily have said she had to go make copies or something. Instead, she followed Bob Larson to his office and sat down with him at a small conference table. In Binghamton, her old girlfriend Terry Scalco had had a chemical dependency evaluation after she got arrested for drunk driving on the way home from the gay disco near her dad's house on Long Island. She'd told Rickie that the chemical dependency counselor who evaluated her came to the conclusion that Terry just needed to slow down a little bit, so Rickie figured that Bob Larson wouldn't find anything wrong with her. Rickie hadn't been doing too well since May, but Terry Scalco was much worse.

Rickie sat down with Bob Larson and was expecting him to ask her if she'd ever had a beer first thing in the morning or if she ever drank an entire six-pack by herself one afternoon and then drove back to the Grand Union for another one. She was ready to say yes or at least not lie flat out, as she figured Terry Scalco had done since Terry Scalco lied about everything.

Instead, Bob Larson was asking her questions about her family, and who didn't have an uncle who was always glugging down a big glass of gin, about getting drunk when you didn't mean to, like the night before that big test in the Milton course at Binghamton, or doing things like stocking up before a long weekend, which Rickie figured everybody did. Bob Larson asked questions and nodded, and then he asked Rickie if she'd hang on for one second while he grabbed something from a file cabinet. Rickie was feeling like this thing was a piece of cake when Bob Larson returned.

"Rickie," he said to her. "There's not a doubt in my mind that you're chemically dependent."

He paused, and she tried not to swallow hard or blink or cry or burst into flames. She nodded and waited for Bob Larson to continue.

"You've got a job, obviously, and a place to stay, so you're what we call in the business 'high functioning.' I've got some suggestions if you want to hear them."

Rickie nodded. Before she even knew what she was doing, she said, "I think I need some suggestions."

Bob Larson's suggestions were simple. "Go to an AA meeting and see how it goes," he said. "Come back and see me next week. Try not to drink."

"OK," she said. "Then what?"

Bob Larson sat back and smiled. "Let's see how you're doing next week."

Not long after Rickie started going to AA meetings and chatting with Bob Larson every week, Rickie got a call at work from Deborah Walker. "It has to do with Tracy Chick," she said. "She's at St. Mary's, and we need to go visit her. Cricket can pick us up at my office, and we'll go."

Tracy Chick had been at St. Mary's before, but this time, she wasn't in the chemical dependency unit. She was all the way upstairs on the top-floor psych ward: the one that was locked.

"Why is she in the psych ward?" Rickie asked Deborah as they rode the elevator to the top floor.

"Why do you think, Rickie Ricardo?" Cricket said.

Rickie opened her mouth, shut it, and closed her eyes for an extra-long moment. It was one thing for Deborah to call her Rickie Ricardo, but it was something else for Cricket to do it, especially when Rickie was wearing nice chino pants, a button-down shirt, and loafers and had just taught a composition class at the downtown community college. Then she looked at Deborah and said, "She had some kind of psychiatric crisis, right? That's usually why a person goes to a psych ward."

Deborah smiled. "That is usually why," she said. She patted Rickie on the arm. "No, really. I don't know what happened to her. Maybe she's depressed? Maybe she had some kind of drug-related psycho freak out? I don't know."

"She's in trouble," Cricket said to Rickie. "And she asked about you."

When the elevator door opened, Rickie caught a whiff of an institutional smell that made her recall the locked psych ward at KU Medical Center. She, Deborah, and Cricket stepped into a little foyer with a row of chairs on one side. On each end of this line of chairs closest to the door was a small table that held a box of tissues. Adjacent to the tissue box was a wide metal door with a small window cut into it. Next to the door was a button mounted in a wall plate. Above it, a sign said, "Press bell to enter," same as the one Rickie had pressed in her days as a Falstaff-delivering pharmacy messenger. She pressed the bell.

"May I help you," said a voice through the little intercom speaker box above the wall plate.

Rickie opened her mouth and nearly said, "Pharmacy messenger."

Deborah stepped forward and said, "Visitors." She paused. "For Tracy Chick."

Rickie tugged on the sleeve of Deborah's jacket. "That's not her name!" she hissed.

"Calm down," said Deborah as the door buzzed them a signal to come in.

Being the child of two headshrinkers whom she'd sometimes visited at work in psych wards, a person might think that Rickie Lynn Jackson would have felt right at home at St. Mary's. Instead, when that big metal security door slammed itself shut behind her, Rickie nearly jumped out of her loafers. She hung back as Deborah marched up to the nurse's desk. She looked around and saw that they were now in a locked waiting room. To the left of the nurse's station was another security door, and to her right was a sharply rectangular couch and two square chairs set up in a small, uncomfortable conversation pit. The door behind the nurse buzzed, and out walked Tracy Chick.

It hadn't been that long since Rickie had last seen Tracy Chick, and it hadn't been much longer than that since she'd been in bed with her. Even so, in that institutional waiting room, with its locked doors and its buzzers and intercoms and that weird chemical fog of incarceration and misery, it took her a minute to recognize the person coming out of that second locked door. Her hair was pulled back in a pony tail, and everything about her was ashen: gray hooded sweat-shirt and sweat pants; gray tints in her blue eyes, gray skin that seemed stretched too tight across her nose and hung too loose from her jaw and chin. The institutional lighting didn't help much, either. Rickie couldn't decide if she looked like she'd aged half a century since she'd last seen her or if ill-fitting, ashen skin came with the crank, or if a pharmacy messenger was delivering her some kind of powerful experi-mental psychotropic drugs, and her look and color were side effects.

Tracy Chick looked at Cricket and then at Deborah and then at Rickie, as if she were trying to place all of them.

"Hi, Tracy," Deborah said. "It's Deborah."

"And Cricket," Cricket added.

"And of course you remember Rickie, right?" Deborah said and nudged Rickie forward.

"Hi, Tracy," Rickie said. She was standing there with her elbows close to her sides and her arms extended about a foot apart, as if she were about to make some kind of wrestling move or offer an invisible plate of hors d'oeuvres. She managed to turn her palms up just enough to make an invitation for a hug or at least a gesture of greeting. Her ears were burning.

"Oh, you silly," Tracy Chick said at last. She moved in to hug Rickie.

"Hi," Rickie said to the side of her head as she hugged her.

"Rickie," she said, as if it were some foreign word she used to know.

"Yes," Rickie said as neutrally as she could. Tracy Chick was looking strangely blank with a tiny hint of wild in the back of her eyes. Her teeth were gray.

"Bedlam," she hissed.

"What about Bedlam?" Deborah said in her best *I'm-trying-to-be-friendly-to-Cricket's-first-girlfriend,-the-fucked-up-junkie-hooker* voice. She sounded almost completely sincere.

Rickie looked at Deborah and then at gray, tense Tracy Chick.

"To Bedlam?" Tracy Chick tried again.

"Bedlam?" Cricket repeated. She sounded exasperated, which made sense to Rickie. She'd been down this road with Tracy Chick before.

"You know what I'm talking about," Tracy Chick insisted. "To Bedlam. Anne Sexton."

"Oh, of course," Rickie said at last. "You are really OK, right?" she said to Tracy Chick. "You mean *To Bedlam and Part Way Back.*"

Tracy Chick exhaled and nodded. "Yes," she said. "That's what it is. Part Way Back. That's me."

"What even is that?" Cricket wanted to know. She had sat down on one of the chairs and was twisting a Kleenex into a thin white rope.

Tracy Chick went to sit down on the couch adjacent to Cricket. "Part way back," she muttered as she sat down.

Rickie followed Tracy Chick and sat next to her. She took Tracy's hand in hers and petted it, the way she'd do with her sister-in-law Nancy's mom, or her gramma on the farm in Nebraska before she died. "She's talking about a book by Anne Sexton," Rickie said as she petted Tracy Chick's hand. "The book is called *To Bedlam and Part Way Back.*"

"She killed herself," Tracy Chick said with perfect pitch

and clarity. "She put on this really nice fur coat, went out to her garage, turned on the car, and lay down in the back seat."

"And the garage door was…" Cricket started.

"Closed," Tracy Chick finished. Tracy Chick looked at Rickie as if she'd seen a vision: a woman wrapped in a fur coat, curled up in the back seat of the car in the dark garage, bound for glory.

•

AFTER THE AA MEETING in the rehab unit at KU Medical Center closed, Rickie headed up to the Cardiac unit, hoping to see CJ sitting up in bed and maybe even talking. She would hold his hand and pet it. Instead, she got another one of those incriminating looks from the nurse when she walked onto the unit.

"Your dad wasn't looking well," said the nurse at the desk. "His blood pressure dropped. I called Dr. Anton."

Before the nurse fully finished her sentence, Rickie said. "What's going on?"

The nurse blinked and inhaled. "OK, I'm telling you what I know. Dr. Anton just called to say he wants to get your dad into the cardiac lab."

Rickie's stomach thumped. "The cardiac lab? For what?"

"The doctor said he thought he could do the procedure with a different contrast dye this time."

"Different dye?" Rickie squeaked. "Why?"

"Dr. Anton can explain later. Your dad's chart says that he wants CPR and all possible measures. Is that right?"

"Yes," she said. "He said it. I thought he'd say no to CPR and everything else and yes to dying, but he said the exact opposite." She paused. "Do everything."

"The cardiac lab is down on the first floor. You'll see the waiting room."

9

Rickie Lynn Jackson wasn't exactly crying, but her eyes were streaming, and her breathing sounded as harsh and loud as a ventilator. It was as if all her organs and guts had slammed shut. She took the stairs as fast as she could and actually jumped the last four steps to the first floor. She landed hard in the stairwell, took a quick breath, and headed for the cardiac lab.

"My dad is here," she said as she approached the desk. She was sweating inside her T-shirt and down the side of her neck. "Dr. Jackson."

The nurse had pushed back in her chair as Rickie made her sweaty, breathless approach, but once Rickie spoke CJ's name, she practically jumped into action.

"Yes," she said. She picked up the phone and pressed a button that beeped somewhere nearby, behind her. "One minute. You're the daughter, right? Dr. Anton is with Dr. Jackson. Our clinic supervisor wants to talk to you."

"OK," Rickie said and tried to take a normal breath. She leaned on the desk for a moment and from her forehead dropped a tiny wet bomb of sweat. "Sorry. I'm sweating all over the place. I rushed down here as fast as I could. Do you know what's going on?"

The nurse clutched the receiver to her chest. "Um, let's see," she said. "Cindy?" She glanced over her shoulder called down the hall.

Just then, a woman in a charcoal suit came out a door. She was groomed in a way that indicated she was not a nurse or a doctor or a technician. Everybody else who worked in the cardiac lab was wearing scrubs. She was obviously from hospital administration: Director of Bad News.

"Hello, I'm Cindy," said the Director of Bad News. "You must be Dr. Jackson's daughter." She came forward a few steps, gave the slightest pause when she saw how sweaty Rickie was, and extended her hand,

"Yes," Rickie said. "Rickie Jackson." She wiped her palm on the back of her shorts and shook Cindy's hand.

"Right this way," she said. She led Rickie through a door into the little room off the waiting area. Cindy Bad News gestured for Rickie to sit down, and then she shut the door.

"How's my dad," Rickie said. She was holding the keys to the Blazer as if they were a talisman, a charm, a miracle cure.

"They're still working on him," Cindy said.

"What do you mean," Rickie said, trying to keep her voice at a somewhat even pitch and speed. "Are they still doing CPR? Did his heart stop again? What happened?"

Cindy held up both hands, palms forward, smiled, and nodded. Evidently, she had been trained to deal with fraught family members of patients who were in big, big trouble. Even so, Rickie was pretty sure she had not had much experience working with a member of a noisy, gesticulating Jewish family, much too experienced in medical emergencies, with some, but not enough, medical knowledge.

"Have you spoken with the doctor yet?" she asked.

"No, I was in a meeting upstairs, and I just got here," Rickie said.

Cindy opened her mouth, closed it, and then spoke. "There was an unexpected complication," she said. She paused.

Rickie nodded. She felt as if some kind of *rigor mortis* were overtaking her.

"The doctor will be right out to talk to you."

"Thanks," she said. She waited for Cindy to stand up and leave, but she didn't. Then Rickie realized that Cindy was sitting in here with her in this room so she wouldn't be alone and freak out and start crawling on the walls and ceiling or scream and cry and upset the people outside who were waiting reasonably for their loved ones to have their routine procedures with no complications.

"So," she said, and smoothed her skirt. "Your dad's a doctor?"

"Yes," Rickie said. She shifted in her seat. "He's retired."

"What was his specialty?"

She took a breath. "Psychiatry," she said. She leaned forward and wiped her temples with a Kleenex. "My mom was a physician, too. Also a psychiatrist."

Cindy's hands stayed on her skirt and her smile didn't move, but Rickie watched Cindy's eyelids rise up. A tiny dent appeared along the side of her nose. "Psychiatrist," she said. She held her breath for a beat, to give Rickie a chance to laugh and say that she was just kidding and that really her mother was a nurse and her dad was a plastic surgeon or a dermatologist.

Rickie nodded.

"That must have been, um, interesting," she said.

Rickie shrugged and waited for Cindy to ask her, as just about everybody from first grade on had done, if her headshrinker parents had done experiments on her and her brother. Cindy kept looking, still slightly wide-eyed and dent-nosed, and said nothing. Rickie was aware that she was sitting there sweating at the cardiac lab because her dad was somnolent and intubated and the medical team in back was probably beating frantically on his chest. Again. Even though she'd just come from an AA meeting and had prayed with her fellow alcoholics for serenity, courage, and wisdom, in this moment, she felt panic, fear, and stupidity. She hated this hospital and everybody in it.

Cindy Bad News stood up and checked her watch. "I'm going to see if I can't flag down the doctor," she said.

Just then, Belushki appeared in the doorway. His scrubs were sweaty around the edges. "Your dad was somnolent," he began. "And we had to intubate him."

"Uh huh," was all Rickie could manage. She pulled up the collar of her T-shirt and wiped her nose and mouth on it.

"Yes," Belushki continued. "But his blood pressure went down and down, and his heart stopped." He paused. "We weren't able to get it going again."

Cindy inhaled through her nostrils, and Rickie understood that CJ had died. She rubbed her nose with her T-shirt and let it go.

"It sounds like he slept himself to death," Cindy said in the gentlest tone. She handed Rickie the box of tissues.

Rickie nodded and took a tissue. "Thanks. I hope so," she said. To Belushksi, she said. "If I'd have known, I'd have said I thought the same procedure, again, was a bad idea, but my dad would have wanted you to go through with it."

"I have to get back," he said. He reached forward and squeezed Rickie's shoulder. "I am truly sorry."

Rickie gave a sob into the tissue.

"He wanted all measures," Cindy said. "It was the right thing." She paused. "Do you need to call anybody? Relatives?"

"Relatives," Rickie repeated and wiped her eyes and nose. "My brother. And my sister-in-law. They're out of the country, but I'll can call them," she said.

"No," Cindy Bad News said gently. "Not yet. Is anybody

here with you? In town? Somebody who could pick you up? Or just come and sit with you?"

Rickie shook her head. It occurred to her, like an elbow to the solar plexus, that she was in her hometown, where she'd been born and grown up, and she was completely alone. "I could call my cousin in Saint Louis," she said.

"Anybody local?" Cindy pressed.

Rickie sat back a moment and thought. Her first and last old boyfriend, Bill DuBois, had quit medical school. Last she heard, he'd gone back to KU and gotten a degree in civil engineering. He was working on a project in La Cygne when Annie died, and he called CJ when he saw the news item in the paper. That was five years ago now, but he was probably around.

Cindy Bad News asked if there was anything more that she could do. Rickie shook her head, and Cindy told Rickie that she could stay in the Bad News Room as long as she wanted, but she should probably go home and try to get some rest. Rickie nodded and squeaked out a wet "Thank you." She blew her nose after Cindy left the room, and then she got up and headed for the door.

On the way to the parking lot, she was making a list in her head of people who'd want to know that CJ had died, starting with Mrs. Levine the neighbor, her Jackson cousins, and some of the relatives in Nebraska. Bill DuBois came to mind again as she got into the Blazer.

As she headed back to CJ's apartment down Rainbow Boulevard, a route so familiar that she wouldn't have to think about it, she figured that yes, Bill Dubois would want to know that CJ had died of a catastrophe in the cardiac lab, but it didn't seem right to call him out of the blue and say, "Oh, hi. I just called to tell you something that will probably be really upsetting to you." She hadn't spoken to him in years, and their relationship was over. She thought it sounded way too bitter to say about somebody like Bill DuBois, "He's dead to me," but in a way he kind of was. She figured that if the relationship is really over and all the feelings have ceased, then the person is deceased. A dead person you miss and wish you could talk to sometimes or get a letter in the mail or sit in a dorm room and talk about literature with, but you know that you simply cannot do any of those things because the person is dead, so you just remember the person and you let that grief and sorrow roll in, like an unexpected wave that soaks your shoes at the beach.

As she neared her old neighborhood, she was thinking about other deceased but not-dead people she knew, and she remembered her old friend, Jill McNally. She and Jill had played softball together and were in French class together and also both worked at KUMC. She was not Rickie's first girlfriend, but they were best friends during their senior year in high school, and they were inseparable. Even so, when Rickie was preparing to go to college far away from Kansas in Binghamton, New York, Rickie didn't think too much about what it might mean to leave behind her friend Jill.

"Are you sure you want to do this?" Jill asked Rickie as they sat side-by-side on the couch in Rickie's playroom in Shawnee Mission and looked at a road atlas. Earlier that day, Jill's hair stylist had streaked her brown hair with black and purple and crafted into this kinetic hairswirl: part beehive and part flat-top. She looked dangerous.

Jill McNally used to go around saying, "Hey, I'm just a nice girl from Kansas" all the time, as if she were some kind of naïve bumpkin and not a straight-A student from a high-end suburb, on her way to a biochemistry degree at KU. She started working in the biochemistry lab at KUMC when Rickie was working there as a pharmacy messenger. They had known each other from French class but weren't really friends until they saw each other in the hospital cafeteria one day. After that, they became lunch break friends and then inseparable friends at school, and then, by the summer after they'd graduated from high school and turned eighteen, the kind of friends who'd sneak into the Westport with the older friends from work. Once Jill got that haircut and decided she wasn't going to join a sorority after all, the bumpkin act was all over.

On that hot August night as they looked at the atlas, they decided that Jill would ride with Rickie to Indianapolis. They'd stay overnight with her brother, and then she'd fly back to Kansas and head off to her biochem program at KU. Rickie would keep driving east and follow the signs to New York.

They didn't have a plan beyond that. Sure, they'd talk on the phone, and OK, they'd write letters, and they'd probably see each other at breaks. But their time together as best friends was just about up. When Rickie took off from Indianapolis with the road atlas on the passenger seat instead of that Jill McNally riding shotgun, she could have been on her way to the Elysian Fields for all either of them knew. Maybe they'd see each other at Thanksgiving; maybe they'd meet up in Heaven. As it turned out, Rickie's parents went on sabbatical to England just after she left for college, so she didn't even go back to Kansas until they returned before the start of her sophomore year. By then, Jill McNally was in an honors program at KU, and she didn't come back to Shawnee Mission from Lawrence, or if she did, she didn't tell Rickie. There wasn't any dramatic split, and while they weren't dead to each other, they weren't exactly alive as friends, either. It was as if their friendship had been put to sleep.

•

RICKIE DID NOT WANT to cause heartbreak or heartache, disrupt anybody's quiet or unquiet slumber, dead or deceased, nor did she want to ruin a flawless moment she'd had in a dream about Jill McNally, right before she left Kansas and they became deceased to each other.

The dream was set in Jill's mom's house in Shawnee Mission. Jill was wearing a light blue shirt with a tab collar. In her dream, Rickie noted that she used to have a shirt exactly like it. Over the shirt, Jill was wearing a letterman sweater, off-white with big silver buttons and navy trim, and also a pair of slim-cut jeans and cordovan loafers, no socks. Her hair was perfect, and she was wearing that bright pink lipstick she always loved. She hugged Rickie.

Rickie used to have dreams about kissing Jill McNally and sometimes actually having sex with her, but in real life, she did not want to cross that border with her best friend. In her dream, she ran her palm up Jill's front, fingered the tab on her collar, and said, "Nice shirt."

Jill said, "Nobody's home. My mom took Mamie to Lawrence." Then she kissed Rickie, full on. In the dream, Rickie was wondering who Mamie was, but it didn't matter. Mamie and Jill's mom had gone to Lawrence, and that meant they'd be away all afternoon. Jill slid her palm up Rickie's T-shirt and then down the front of her running shorts, and she led her backwards to her childhood bed.

At the end of the dream, it took Rickie a second to get her bearings. At Binghamton, once she'd raised the curtain and stepped out as a lesbian, she'd talk about Jill McNally, and people like Deborah Walker would say, "Was she your first girlfriend?" Nobody could believe that they'd never had sex, never even kissed, and even Rickie sometimes wondered if her friendship with Jill had died of unrequited love. In that dream, though, the two of them just being there together, in that dreamtime afternoon while everybody was away, was enough. When the dream ended, Rickie realized that the feeling she had was the closest thing to closure she was likely to get. Now, driving back to Shawnee Mission in the Blazer, Rickie didn't want to call Jill, after all those years of peace, and wreck that feeling with news about her father's death.

10

THE PHONE WAS RINGING in CJ's apartment when Rickie walked in. She dropped the tote bag of CJ's clothes on the floor and picked up the receiver. On the other end, Tom was crying and said he'd gotten a weird feeling and called the hospital just after CJ had died.

"I'm not sure what I'm supposed to do," Rickie wailed. The second she heard Tom's voice, she had started bawling, and now there was no reason to stop.

Nancy, Tom's wife, took the receiver. "It's OK," she said, in the soothing tone of a lion tamer. "It's OK. Tom and I are at the airport in New Zealand now. We'll be back late tomorrow, and we'll all take care of CJ. You don't have to do anything now, Rickie. It's OK."

•

WHEN RICKIE CALLED THE Cremation Society the next day to ask if she and Tom and Nancy could have a viewing, the funeral director she spoke to was soothing and professional.

"Hello," he said. "My name is Bruce Bishop. Of course we could arrange a viewing for you. Just so you know, it's an extra ninety-five dollars."

It seemed to Rickie that she and Tom and Nancy could just go over to the morgue at KU and have them pull him out of the drawer, easy as taking a big loaf of bread from the oven. Even so, haggling with Bruce Bishop over ninety-five bucks seemed wrong.

"All right," she said at last. "We'll come tomorrow morning."

"OK, why don't you come at 9:30 tomorrow, and we'll take

care of some paperwork?" said Bruce Bishop. "Then you can have the viewing and spend all the time you need with him."

She looked at the calendar on the wall above the phone. "How much time will we need for the paperwork?"

"The paperwork will take about a half an hour. Will that work for you?"

Rickie was thinking, "I just want to see him, say good-bye, kiss his forehead, and take a picture."

Bruce Bishop was thinking, *I just want my ninety-five dollars and the cremation fee.*

At last, Rickie said, "Yes. Thank you very much. See you tomorrow."

•

THE NEXT MORNING, TOM, Nancy, and Rickie went in together and stopped at the front desk. A receptionist looked at them and smiled.

Tom clicked into his business mode.

"I'm Thomas Jackson," he said. "We're here to see Dr. Jackson, our dad."

"And who's your funeral director?" asked the receptionist. She nodded and smiled, as if they were there for a family portrait.

"Bruce Bishop," Rickie said. "I spoke to him yesterday."

"Bruce, Junior or Bruce, Senior?" The receptionist wanted to know.

"Not sure," she said. "He sounded like he was about my age, if that helps."

"Oh yes," she said, and she pointed to a line of photos on the wall. They were headshots of the funeral directors. One was a young woman; one was a white guy who looked to be about their age—somewhere between Rickie and Tom and Nancy, and two old white guys with silver hair and wire rim glasses, probably of Annie and CJ's vintage. "Bruce Bishop, Junior. I'll ring him."

Bruce Bishop, Junior, came right out and looked as if he'd walked right out of the yearbook photo gallery from Shawnee Mission High School, anytime between 1977 and 1983. His hair was still mostly brown, side-parted and neatly combed. He wore a nice navy suit, light blue shirt, and blue-and-red striped tie.

"Good morning," Bruce Junior said. "You must be the Jackson family. I want to offer my condolences."

He shook hands with each of them, and they followed him into a conference room.

They sat down at the conference table, and Rickie extracted a manila folder from her bag. Nancy raised her eyebrows and smiled.

"Is that Nancy's funeral flow chart?" Tom asked.

"Of course it is," Nancy said.

Tom laughed, and Rickie did, too. Then Rickie turned to Bruce Junior who was smiling somewhat uncomfortably. "Nancy plans everything," Rickie said to him.

"OK, then," Bruce Junior said, and he put his palms on the table. "Why don't we get started?"

•

WHEN THE FORMS WERE completed, Bruce Junior started selling. "What might you need for the memorial service?" he asked. "I can show you some guestbooks."

Tom and Rickie looked at each other, and Rickie could tell they were both thinking they could stop off at the drug store and pick up a notebook.

"Let's just get a nice one," Tom said, as if he could hear Nancy saying that they could not buy cheap spiral notebook from the drug store.

Bruce Junior got up and took a small stack of guest books off a sideboard near the conference table. "How about one of these?" He held up one with a big American flag embossed on the cover. "Was your dad a veteran?"

"He was in the Navy," Tom said.

"Yes," Rickie said. "But that's a little too patriotic."

Tom and Nancy giggled, and even Bruce Junior gave Rickie a tiny smile. "Plain blue, then?"

"Perfect."

"How about keepsake urns?" He wanted to know.

"Keepsake urns," Rickie said. "What's that?"

"You know," Tom said. "That little eagle CJ keeps on Annie's desk?"

"That *chotchkie* has ashes in it?" Rickie said. "That's kind of weird."

"It is weird," Tom said. "But CJ loved it. Actually, I would like some of CJ's ashes."

"Really?" Rickie said. "Should we both have some? In *chotchkies*?"

"I know what we can do," Tom said to Bruce Bishop. "Can we take our mom's ashes, mix them with some of our dad's ashes, and put them in separate little urns?"

"Absolutely," Bruce Junior said.

It seemed to Rickie that this ash-mixing and keepsake urn *chotchkie* project would sound completely bizarre and maybe blaphemous or possibly unsanitary to a guy who worked in a family funeral home, but Bruce Junior was imperturbable.

"We've got one eagle *chotchkie*," Tom continued. "Can we get another eagle? Then both of us can have an eagle."

Bruce Junior was already checking his list. "The eagles are out of stock," he said. "We've got these rectangular marble keepsake urns in several colors." From a drawer in the sideboard he took out what looked like a tiny marble coffin.

"That's nice," Tom said.

"Kind of creepy," Rickie said. "It looks like a coffin. I like the eagle better. Are there any other kinds of *chotchkies*? Figures?"

"How about this," Tom said to Bruce Junior. "Can you inscribe their names and an eagle on the side of the coffin?"

"Certainly," Bruce Junior said.

It occurred to Rickie that the engraved eagle coffin *chotchkies* were going to cost a fortune. Tom would point out that CJ would say he didn't care how much it cost. Then they'd all remember that CJ and Annie were dead, and they'd sit there in an unusual silence, or else they'd all start bawling. Rickie figured she'd wait until she saw the bill.

Bruce Junior worked at his calculator. "Here's an itemized list," he announced. He started with the cremation services, which cost twelve hundred bucks. Then the ninety-five bucks for the viewing, twenty for the non-partisan funeral guest book, and five hundred for the two engraved keepsake urns. Rickie thought it was ridiculous to pay that much for a *chotchkie* full of ashes, but it seemed even more ridiculous to stand on principle. This was it. There were no more parents to cremate. CJ was somewhere in the building at that moment. They'd take one last look at him, and then there'd be nothing left but ashes. CJ's checkbook was sitting on the table. As the trustee, Rickie could sign the checks, and his friends at the bank would clear them. It was his money. CJ was still footing the bill.

Rickie realized that Bruce Junior had given her the invoice. He and Tom and Nancy were waiting for her to look at it and write the check.

"OK," she said. "Cremation services, viewing, guest book,

engraved keepsake urns." She looked around at her brother. He nodded. She signed the invoice and passed it to Bruce Junior. Then she reached for CJ's checkbook.

After they finished our transaction, Bruce Junior stood up. "Let's go downstairs for the viewing," he said. "Are you ready?"

Rickie looked at Tom and felt her eyes widening. The funeral arrangements had been easy enough. Even the negotiations for the eagle *chotchkies* had not been very taxing, really. But now they were going to have a last look at their dead dad. Tom raised his eyebrows at Rickie and Nancy, and Nancy smiled and nodded. Rickie took a deep breath and followed them out of the conference room.

As they followed Bruce Junior down the thoroughly vacuumed stairs and into an anteroom that was equally spotless in floor, walls, and furniture. The cleanliness and order made her uneasy. Maybe it was too much Hollywood or too many classroom discussions of Poe stories, but she kept expecting to feel nitre drip on her head, to come upon a rampart of bones, to hear the grisly tinkling of bells coming from somebody's fool's cap. This place was as clean as a clinic. Bruce Junior opened a door to what looked to be a very well-appointed exam room. "He's in here," he said.

Bruce Junior left, and Tom, Nancy, and Rickie went into the exam room. There was CJ, lying on a gurney with a fuzzy maroon blanket pulled up to his chin. His glasses were off, and his eyes were closed. His hair looked whiter than it had in life, and they'd put a lot of make up on his face. He looked like an expertly groomed simulacrum of himself taking a nap.

"Hi, CJ," Rickie said, and she touched the blanket. When she'd visited him in the ICU, intubated and unconscious, he looked more dead than he did in that moment. Then she kissed his forehead. It was completely cold, as if he'd been transformed into a life-sized ice cream cake. "He's cold," she said to Tom.

Tom and then Nancy kissed CJ's forehead and agreed that CJ was cold. Then they all looked at each other, wondering what to do next.

"I want to take a picture of him," Rickie said, and she took out a disposable camera.

"I do, too." Tom pulled the same kind of disposable camera from his jacket pocket. "Is that wrong?"

"Wrong, how?"

"Is it disrespectful?" Tom said. "I don't think it is, is it?" His camera was already in his hand, pointed at somnolent, chilly CJ.

Rickie shrugged and said, "I don't think CJ would think it's disrespectful. He was always taking pictures."

"That is the truth," said Nancy.

"Think of it this way," Rickie said. "CJ was taking pictures of us when we were tiny babies, naked in the bathtub. Now we're taking pictures of him at the other end of life. It's a family tradition."

Tom lifted his palms. "*Abie gazint*," he said.

They made like paparazzi with their cheap cameras, and then Tom checked his watch.

"Do you want some private time with CJ," Tom asked in a slightly quavering voice. "I do."

Rickie's stomach sank. "I do, and I don't," she said. "I mean, this whole thing is starting to freak me out."

"Rickie," Tom said. "I know this is freaky. But this is the last time we'll see him. Don't you want some time with CJ?"

"You all stay here," she said. "I've had time with him. I mean, we talked when he was in the hospital." She looked at

Tom and Nancy, then at CJ, all cold and dead under his nap blanket. Nancy stepped forward and put her hand between Rickie's shoulder blades. Rickie leaned over the gurney and kissed CJ's cold forehead one last time. She opened her mouth to say something, but her voice cracked, and she paused. She cleared her throat and tried one more time. "Bye, CJ." She laid her hand on his solar plexus, just above his dogged heart. "Love you," she added.

She paused again, overwhelmed by the moment's weirdness. She loved her dad, but she'd never said, "I love you" straight to his face, and she didn't remember him ever saying it to her, either. Under that blanket, he was inert and cold. She was full of a warm soup of sorrow, grief, loss, and fear with a dollop of relief. She put her forehead on his dead, hard chest and sobbed.

Nancy patted her back, and Rickie rested her head for an extra moment. She knew that if Tom had done what Rickie just did, Rickie would have run out of the room. Tom was the big brother, though, and watching Rickie cry was nothing new to him. He sniffed, and then he patted her on the back, gently pulled her upright, and gave her an immobilizing, double-arm hug.

Rickie took one more sobbing breath, and then she calmed down enough to grab a tissue, blow her nose, wipe her eyes, and speak in nearly normal tones. "I really do think I'll go upstairs now," she said. "You can have some time with him. Then should we to to Cosentino's? Grab some lunch and start going through stuff?"

"OK, Rickie," Tom said, as gentle as he'd have been with a wild animal. He patted her back. "We'll have some time with him, and then we'll find you upstairs."

She gripped her brother's arm and patted cold, dead,

napping CJ one last time. Then she hurried up the winding staircase to the waiting room. She paused a second, and then she headed out the door to the parking lot. The morning was warm but not oppressive yet, and she stood by the door of the Blazer for a moment. The building at the far side of the parking lot had a huge chimney crawling up its back, up, up into the sky. Nothing was coming out of it. After Tom and Nancy finished saying good-bye to CJ, Bruce Junior would wheel CJ's gurney out the back door of the exam room, down a hall, through a tunnel, and into that back building with the big chimney.

She knew the story after that. CJ had decreed cremation as his choice, but even so, it seemed wrong to send one more Jewish guy to an oven, up a chimney. She rubbed her nose and stayed there, leaning against the car for another second and thought about what she could do to make herself feel better. She could open up the back of the Blazer, put the back seats down, and wheel CJ right in off the gurney. Then she could drive out to the country, dig a big hole for CJ, and bury him in a plain pine box.

She was rubbing her palms together, imagining the blisters she'd get from digging the grave. At that moment, Tom and Nancy came out the front door of the Cremation Society and said, "There you are."

11

"Not yet, but pretty soon, will you put in a change of address so that CJ's mail goes to your house?" Tom asked when they walked into the tiny kitchen at CJ's apartment.

Rickie stopped in her tracks, still holding the bag of cold cuts, cheese, pickles, cole slaw, and bread from Cosentino's. "Oh," she said. "I guess that makes sense once we empty out this apartment."

She put the bag of lunch on the kitchen table and then sat down and flipped through the most recent pile of mail. From it, she extracted a white glossy magazine. "Check this out," she said to Tom and Nancy, who were unpacking the lunch supplies and getting out plates. "I've been reading CJ's *New England Journal of Medicine,*"

"What for?" Tom said and laughed as he put plates, forks, and knives on the table.

"I like those 'Case Records of the Massachusetts General Hospital.' They're like detective stories."

Tom nodded. "I like those, too. I read them at work sometimes."

"Did you read that one about the guy with the back pain and vision loss or something and the rash?"

"The syphilis guy?"

Rickie raised her hand and smacked it on the new issue. "I knew it was syphilis! I knew it!"

"The rash was a dead giveaway."

"Yes, but the authors made it sound like they'd never heard of a man having sex with men and not telling his wife about it. I mean, you'd think it was a Case Record of the Massachusetts General Hospital from 1984 or something."

Tom looked at her for a second and turned to the refrigerator.

"I've got CJ's medical license here," Rickie said as she scanned the cover contents of CJ's precious journal. "I've got his driver's license, too."

"What are you talking about?"

"His license. And his ID. I'll get his mail now. I sign checks with his name on the account. I'm a, what do you call that?" She paused and waited for the literary term to bubble up. "I'm a palimpsest. A palimpsest."

Tom looked at her and frowned.

"You know," she said. "It's a picture of somebody."

"I know, I know." Tom waved at her. "You can see the image of somebody else underneath it. Vocabulary word. Spelling bee."

"Yes! That's it. What I'm saying is I'm CJ's palimpsest." She stopped and cocked her head. "Is that the right usage? I'm the image below CJ," she continued. "Though I think it would work better if CJ were actually the image below me."

"Where is this going?"

"I was thinking I've got all the stuff here. I could just be a doctor. I mean, look. License. ID. Journals. Look at this." She picked up a package, about the size of an envelope, wrapped in plastic. "'Exam gloves. Introductory offer: ten boxes per case. You may mix sizes in a case. We bill you or use a credit card. Free clock with first order.' Look! There's a trial set inside this pack. I'm ready to go."

"What about malpractice insurance?"

She slapped down the gloves and glared at Tom. "Are you kidding?" she said. "You don't think CJ's paid up through the next expiration date, whenever that is?"

Tom laughed and shook his head. "You can't be serious. What are you going to do? Write prescriptions?"

Rickie frowned. "Well, probably not," she said. "But I could see patients. Don't you remember what Annie said about why she switched from pediatrics to psychiatry? Remember? She said the parents of her patients just wanted to talk."

"Right," Tom said. "She switched to psych so she could mostly just talk to people."

"Exactly," Rickie said and slapped the gloves down again. "That is what I'm saying. I could just talk to people. Or just listen to people talk."

"About what? What if you get somebody who is actually sick? Why am I even talking about this?"

"Don't be such a dud, Tom," Rickie said. "I'm just saying it would be fun to set up a practice and be a doctor."

"Yeah, Tom," Nancy interjected. She was busy making sandwiches, but she was not missing a second. "Don't be a dud."

He frowned. "What would you call yourself?"

"Chucky Joe?" Rickie said. Everybody laughed. "No," she continued. "How about this: Charles Joseph Rickie Lynn Jackson, MD. Dang!"

Tom shook his head. "Never mind the fact that you are not a man. What are you going to do about all the people who still call you Rickie?"

"I am not a man," she explained. "I am a person with many names. Think of the Royal Family. Lots of those people had many names. King Edward the Eighth had about a million names. The last name in the string was David, and that's what they called him in the family. But in public he was King Edward. King George was Albert Frederick Arthur George, right? They called him Bertie."

"Are you going to be the King of England as well as a doctor?"

"She could," Nancy speculated.

"Thank you, Nancy, " Rickie said. "But seriously. I could pass as CJRL Jackson, MD. That's a lot of initials. People will understand that I have a load of names, and it's just easy to pick one out of the middle. Call me Rickie. It's not that complicated. I knew a guy in graduate school who had a different name every semester."

"How could he do that?" Nancy asked.

"Easy. He showed up as Jimmy Len Windsor. By the end of the first semester, he was James Windsor. Then he discovered that his Portuguese grandmother, whose last name was Rocha, may have been Jewish. By the end of the second semester, he was James Rocha, and he was Jewish. When he graduated, he had them put Diego Leon Rocha on his diploma. I don't think Jimmy Len Windsor ever appeared anywhere ever again. Everybody just took it in stride. I called him Jimmy, and then James, and then Diego, and so did everybody else. *Luz il leben*, right?"

Tom gave her a long look to make sure she was done, and then he shook his head. "We have to get this apartment cleaned up." He stopped and eyed her "You better not get yourself in trouble with malpractice," he said. "Or prescriptions. I mean, don't be stupid."

•

As they were eating lunch, Bruce Junior from Cremation Society called. Tom wanted CJ's glasses, and Bruce Junior had found them at the last minute. Rickie said she'd drive over in the Blazer and pick them up. Tom and Nancy were jet lagged and went into CJ's room to take a nap.

At the Cremation Society, the secretary handed Rickie

CJ's glasses just as they were, frames somewhat askew from the thumpings and proddings and hasty removals of them in the past several days. She laid them carefully on the passenger seat of the Blazer, and then took them up to CJ's apartment and set them down, earpieces up as CJ had taught her to do, on the coffee table. Then she sat down on the couch to write the piece about CJ that she'd read at the memorial service they'd have in a couple of days.

Since she was not a physician, not even a quack, really, she turned to literature for palliative care. Virginia Woolf's *Mrs. Dalloway* had come to mind after the discussion about the code status when CJ knew he was looking at the end of his life, and the end saddened him. She'd found a copy in the reading room downstairs, and now she reached for the book and flipped to the already-marked page in which Clarissa is listening for Big Ben. She rested on Woolf's use of the word "irrevocable." Annie always pronounced the big word with the accent on the third syllable: irr-re-*voc*-able. CJ did, too, on most days, but he preferred the British pronunciation: irr-*revo*-cable. Rickie decided to pronounce it the CJ way.

She kept reading Woolf's encomium, as she'd done probably seven other times in her life already. Once again, she felt surprised and moved by Woolf's love of life. She figured a person wouldn't expect somebody who got completely depressed and walked into a river with a pocket full of stones to write something as uplifting as "Heaven only knows why one loves it so." But she knew. Clarissa Dalloway knew, and so did Rickie's parents, now both dead: people love life.

Rickie didn't always feel that way herself, and a lot of people she knew who survived the 1980s would say the same thing. But Woolf knew it, Clarissa knew it, Annie and CJ knew it, and on pretty good days, she knew it, too: people love life. Annie did not want to die when that idiot ran her over in the crosswalk. CJ did not want to die of bad heart trouble and worse doctor trouble. He wanted to live, and so did Annie. Rickie didn't think either CJ or Annie ever read *Mrs. Dalloway* while they were busy loving life, but they would have recognized Clarissa. Rickie put the book down, went to the den and pulled the sleeping bag up to her nose.

•

THE NEXT DAY, Tom, Nancy, and Rickie agreed it was a good day to start organizing CJ's stuff. They'd already divvied up the furniture, so the aim was to put color-coded stickers on things and get them ready for the movers to transport to Saint Louis and Dyke Heights, Minneapolis, and arrange whatever else was left for donations.

Rickie decided to start in the walk-in closet, clearing out the armoire and packing up clothes in big black garbage bags to take to the nearby donation center in what used to be a grocery store in their old neighborhood. She opened up the double doors to the armoire and took a quick survey of the contents of the shelves and drawers: innumerable pairs of socks, boxer shorts, T-shirts, and knit shorts.

"Last chance, Tom," Rickie yelled from the closet. "Have you looked through CJ's stuff in here? Need boxers, socks, or T-shirts?"

"No," Tom called from across the bedroom. "I don't need any of that stuff."

"Just *vorf* it," Nancy said.

"All right," Rickie said, and she shook a big black garbage bag until it wafted open. The socks were in the top drawer of the armoire, so she started chucking them quickly into the open-mouthed bag. When she and Tom and Nancy had cleaned out Annie's bathroom for the last time, they did the same thing with her bathroom drawers: they chucked the contents before they could really think about what they were doing. Like maniacs, they tossed out her dozens of barely used lipsticks, her perfume, her tweezers and razors and toothbrush. It was the last of her, and they knew it. Rickie tried not to feel that familiar nauseous wave as she scooped up armloads of CJ's white socks and dumped them in the big black garbage bag.

In the middle of the sock drawer, she extracted CJ's old handball glove, still wrapped around a handball. The whole kit was still in pretty good condition. A person who wanted to play handball could probably have put on the glove, flexed and stretched his or her fingers and hands a few times, and proceeded to whack the ball. She didn't know anybody who played handball nor where she might find a handball court in the event that she felt like whacking the ball a few times by herself. She put the ball glove on the edge of one of the upper shelves, and then she set out with both hands to finish the sock drawer.

In the last giant scoop of socks, she came up with a well-worn flat silver case, about the size of a switchplate cover. It had hinges on the side, and the top cover was engraved with the initials EVJ.

"Hey," she called out as she turned from the armoire and headed for the living room. "Look at this. EVJ. Isn't that Eileen?"

"What is it?" Tom asked.

"It looks like some kind of case," Rickie said. "Cigarette case? Very mid-century."

"What does the V stand for?" Nancy asked.

"Let's see," Tom said. "What was her name? Eileen Virginia Jackson?"

"Eileen Virginia!" Nancy exclaimed. "Could it be more *goyische*?"

"I know," Tom said. "But so were all the other names of CJ's siblings," Tom noted. "Marty, Kenny, Jimmy."

"Marty, Kenny, and Jimmy don't sound that *goyische* to me," Rickie said. "Maybe Jimmy does."

"Tom is not a very Jewish name," Nancy pointed out.

"Yes," Rickie said. "Unless you count Doubting Thomas, I can't think of a single Jew named Tom. *Goyische*."

"I bet Becky Jackson would know for sure what Eileen's middle name was," Tom said.

"Becky might know," Rickie said, "but Esti Jackson will know for sure. She's got a lot of documents and family history." She snapped the case open and shut. "I don't smoke and won't use it, but this case thing is cool. I'm going to keep it. I want something of Eileen's."

"You never knew her, though, did you?" Nancy said.

"She died when CJ was still in college," Tom said.

"I feel like I know her, though," Rickie said. She fingered the cigarette case. "I mean, did I tell you about that mole on my leg last fall?"

"Mole on your leg?" Nancy said.

"I told you about the mole, Tom." Rickie said. She looked at Nancy. "I thought I told you, too. Anyway, you know about Eileen's leg, right?"

Nancy frowned. "Of course. She's the one who had a tumor in her leg, and the doctors wanted to amputate it, but she said no."

"Right," Rickie said. "Eileen had osteosarcoma. I had this mole on the back of my calf. It was kind of funny look-ing, like a little cluster of freckles. It's one of those things I never remembered to ask my doctor about, but then when I went in for a sore Achilles tendon last fall, the doctor spotted it and said it looked funny. She gave me a referral to a dermatologist."

"And the dermatologist wanted to amputate your leg?" Nancy said.

"What?" Tom said from the other side of the room where he was packing up a bag of T-shirts. "What are you saying?"

"No, no," Rickie said. "But it's funny. It really is funny because I really thought…"

"You thought the dermatologist was going to cut off your leg because of a mole?"

Rickie waved her arms. "No, no. No. I'm saying the dermatologist took a little snick of the mole and sent it in for a biopsy. I got a call a few days later, on a Friday afternoon, and the nurse left a message saying, 'It's not an emergency.' I figured it was nothing. I mean, I wasn't even going to call back. Then, the following Monday, the nurse called again."

"So it wasn't nothing," Nancy said.

"No. I mean, yes. It wasn't nothing. The nurse told me, 'It's a severely atypical mole.' I was shocked!"

"I'd be shocked, too," Nancy said.

"It wasn't cancer, though," Tom said. He rustled a trash bag.

Rickie continued. "No. That's true. It wasn't cancer. 'Severely atypical' sounds like something godawful, but the nurse explained that it just meant a really weird mole. But the doctor wanted to take it off. I said to the nurse, 'Will it turn into cancer?' The nurse said, 'Only .05 percent of severely atypical moles turn into cancer.' I said, 'Yes, but it'd be really horrible to die of a mole.'"

"You said that?" Nancy said.

Rickie looked at Nancy, then Tom, then Nancy. She was going to laugh, but then she didn't. "Well," she said at last. "I did say that. After the words left my mouth, a pall of silence fell on the conversation."

"No kidding," Tom said.

"What happened?" Nancy asked.

"OK," Rickie said, and she snapped Eileen's cigarette case and waved it. "That's the Eileen part. I made the appointment to get my severely weird atypical mole snicked off. They call it an excision, which to me sounded seriously horrible."

"It wasn't that bad, though," Tom said. "CJ had a bunch of those basal cell things cut off his back. They really had to dig those things out."

"I know," Rickie said. "I read about the procedure in a brochure they gave me, and it didn't sound that bad. A little cut, a little scrape, a few stitches, done. But here's the thing."

"What?" Tom and Nancy said together.

"All I could think about was Eileen getting her leg amputated. I was thinking, 'I just made an appointment to get a mole excised ten days from now. I wonder if Eileen made an appointment to get her leg amputated and then changed it.'"

"Yes, but she never did get her leg amputated," Tom said. "And the cancer spread and killed her."

Rickie snapped Eileen's case again. "I know, I know," she said. "But it was just the thought of it: the mole, the cancer, Eileen and her leg. It's funny how I think about Eileen all the time, and I never even knew her."

"Look on the wall," Nancy said. She was pointing to a photo of Eileen. "Look at her. She was probably still in high school when this photo was taken—a cheerleader, a member of the glee club, an officer in the drama club. She was a kid, but she looked like a fully composed, grown-up adult woman. She was a star."

"I know," Rickie said. "And then she got sick. I wonder

how she found out about the cancer. What she was doing when she learned? How did she feel about it? When I got home from the dermatologist, I kept thinking about how she might have felt, knowing that she was going to go in and have her leg amputated. I read about the procedure, and it's not that complicated, but can you imagine? Imagine waking up from that surgery. Your leg is gone, and it must hurt like hell. I mean, even with drugs, how could you stand it? And then you have no leg!"

Tom rolled his eyes.

Rickie waved off her brother. To Nancy, she said, "It scared me. I'm not kidding. I made another call to the dermatologist and arranged to have the mole removed the next day."

"Did you really?" Nancy said.

"Of course she did," Tom said. "She was in a panic, especially after she read about osteosarcoma and leg amputation, probably late at night."

"I was in a panic." Rickie nodded this time. "I really was." She snapped Eileen's case once more. "I went in, and the doctor cut out the mole in about three seconds."

"Did it hurt?"

"Not right then," Rickie said. "But it did bother me afterwards. It looked and felt like I'd been bit by a dog."

"Better a dog bite than an amputation," Tom said. He left the room with his trash bag full of CJ's T-shirts.

"Did it leave a scar?"

She nodded and turned her calf out so Nancy could see it. "It did," she said. "It still itches. Whenever I look at it, I think of Eileen."

Tom returned to CJ's room, and Rickie followed. Tom picked up the handball glove. It was curled like a relic on the shelf.

"This is cool," he said. "But who plays handball?"

"You know," Rickie said as she leaned down and tugged on the big drawer at the very bottom of CJ's gigantic armoire. "Deborah Walker's dad plays handball. Racquetball, too, but he plays handball at the JCC." She paused and tugged at the heavy drawer. "Jesus," she exclaimed. "Oh, for Christ's sake."

A trove of porn videos came into view.

"What?" said Tom. "More relics?"

"No," she said. "It's something else." She grabbed a garbage bag. "His porn collection."

"What?" Tom said again, this time incredulous. "Porn collection?"

"Porn collection?" Nancy echoed.

Rickie nodded and shook out the garbage bag. "It's like something out of a Philip Roth novel."

"Just a second," Tom said. He raced out of the bedroom, down the hall to the bathroom.

"What's he doing?" Nancy said as she came into CJ's room. "Is there a shredder for these papers?"

Just then, Tom returned. He was wearing one of those respirator masks that CJ had worn outside sometimes on cold winter days, and he'd slipped on the pair of rubber gloves that were under the sink in the bathroom. "I'm ready," he said.

•

AFTER TOM DUMPED THE bag of CJ's porn down the garbage chute at the end of the corridor and returned to CJ's apartment, they all sat down in the living room.

"Let's pack up this stuff now and decide what we want shipped. Then we have to get ready for the memorial service," Nancy said.

"Rickie, where can we donate the clothes?" asked Tom.

"The donation center over by Trailwood School," she said. "I can take a load now."

"Fine," said Tom and Nancy.

"Make sure you keep track of what's in the bags," Tom said. "We can deduct the donations from CJ's taxes."

"Good plan," Rickie said. "Also, you all need to send me your expenses. Car, meals, whatever. Whatever CJ used to pay for when you came to visit, OK?"

"That's right," said Nancy. "You can deduct them as funeral expenses from the estate taxes."

"Oh," Rickie said. "Good point. Yes. So, send me your expenses and add up a total, and I'll write a check and send it back. Sound good?"

"Rickie," Tom said. "You're the Bank of CJ now."

They all laughed. "I know," she exclaimed. "Who'd have thought?"

It was funny because Tom was not only the older brother, but he'd always been level-headed and responsible about money and managing things. She'd been surprised when Annie and CJ did their estate planning, and they told Rickie that they'd made her the executor. Annie never gave an explanation, but Rickie always suspected that Annie put her down as the executor because she wanted to give Rickie a role in the family so that she'd come home and feel part of things when somebody died.

"OK," said Nancy. "And remember, we're going to go through those boxes of slides and photos at Christmas, right? Jewish Christmas in Saint Louis? I'll ask your cousins to come."

"Is that OK with you?" Rickie asked them both. "We did Jewish Christmas at your house last year."

"Sure," Tom said. He looked at Nancy, and she nodded.

"We like having everybody," she said. She didn't say "We're all that's left," but Rickie felt it.

The light in CJ's apartment was beginning to dim, and his twelfth-floor living room and kitchen windows opened up on the sun setting on Shawnee Mission, sprawling and stretching to the south, recumbent under a thin cover of billboards and long strips of highways, roads, and freeways. The day settled: a shroud, a cloud of ashes, a scrim of dust.

12

THE SERVICE FOR CJ was nice, but the burden of grief was heavier than it had been with Annie. Nobody missed a cue or made a scene, but nobody's heart was in it, not really. It felt like a re-run. Most of the same people who had attended Annie's memorial service, in this same chapel, nearly five years earlier, had now gathered to say farewell to CJ. The fact that he went to an outpatient clinic for a routine angiogram and was picked up from the morgue by the Cremation Society, dead as a doornail, evoked all the sorrow and irony of Annie's death. The fact that nobody would ever have thought that CJ would get caught up in a colossal cardio-catastrophe sharpened the pain point. Everybody wanted to show up and pay their respects to CJ and the family and get out as fast as they could.

For the recessional, Rickie, Tom, and Nancy had agreed that they should play something from CJ's favorite recording of all times, *Ella Fitzgerald Sings the Cole Porter Songbook.* Mrs. Levine's daughter Joanie had copied the album onto a cassette, and Joanie brought a big boombox to play in the chapel. Tom thought they should play "Ev'ry Time We Say Goodbye." Rickie had voted for the Neneh Cherry version of "I Got You Under My Skin," but everybody nixed her pick. There had been some serious consideration of "It's De-Lovely," but in the end they went with "I Get a Kick Out of You."

At the end of the service, without meaning to, without practice and without even a cue beyond Joanie Levine pushing a button on a boombox, everybody began singing: not just Tom and Rickie, who'd grown up with Ella Fitzgerald singing Cole Porter, but Nancy and Cousins Becky and Esti, and Deborah Walker, who'd caught a flight to Kansas City for the service and was flying back to Minneapolis the next day, and everybody else who'd ever listened to Ella Fitzgerald ever in their lives. Everybody sang along. When they reached the end of the song, their voices cracked and people's eyes streamed. Everybody clapped when it was over.

•

AFTER THE SERVICE, RICKIE's cousin Esti was talking to her about the relatives. Esti wasn't telling Rickie anything she didn't know, but hearing it all at once made the family health past seem dismal and the prospects for present and future family members look bleak. Rickie gulped and changed the subject.

"OK, tell me this," she said. "CJ always said that the worst event of his childhood was that he didn't get a bar mitzvah because his family was too poor. Did Marty or Kenny or Jimmy have a bar mitzvah?"

"Hmmm," Esti said. "I don't think so. My dad told me that the family moved from Topeka to Monticello, New York in the spring before the fall that he turned thirteen. He said he didn't want to have to start over with a new rabbi in Monticello, so he just never got a bar mitzvah. He used to say he'd been an agnostic since 1938, which would have been that year."

"How about the other brothers?"

"I don't think so. If Marty didn't, then I doubt Kenny would have. He was only a year younger than Marty. As for Jimmy, I don't think he did, either."

"I think you are right," Rickie said. "I talked to our cousin

Timothy this morning, when he called to offer condolences and ask about a bill for a *Yahrzeit* contribution and upkeep for the graves at Mount Hope Cemetery. He said to me, 'I don't know what this yare-zeet thing is. I just don't know anything about the Jewish religion.'"

"Yes," Esti said. "I don't think any of them ever got a bar mitzvah. You didn't have a bat mitzvah, did you?"

"Hell, no," Rickie said. "I probably could have if I'd wanted to, but I didn't want to go to Hebrew school. Tom didn't go to Hebrew school, either, though he converted later. He ended up getting one of those quick-and-dirty bar mitzvahs in Israel that time he and Nancy went to Tel Aviv for Nancy's dad's birthday."

"Marty always said it wasn't a big deal, not getting a bar mitzvah," Esti said. "But I'm not so sure. Not long before he died, he was telling me about a colleague's mom who'd gotten her bat mitzvah at age eighty-one. 'Why not?' she said. Marty thought that was the best thing he'd heard in ages. But then his heart gave out, and that was that."

"Did your mom ever talk about it? The No Bar Mitzvah Syndrome?" Rickie asked Esti. Esti's mom was a shrink, after all, and had actually trained as an analyst. "I mean, do you think the brothers had some kind of inferiority complex? Like they weren't really men?"

Esti laughed. "I'm not sure about Jimmy or Kenny, and you'd know about CJ better than I would. For my dad, it was about his parents being poor. Possibly poor and cheap. I think after that, he associated being Jewish with being poor and cheap, and he did not want to be poor. Or cheap. I don't think CJ did, either."

"I think you're right about that."

"But here's the catch," Esti said. "I did some research on

the bat mitzvah and the bar mitzvah. They are coming of age rituals."

"Yes, I know that," Rickie said.

"But did you know that the coming of age part is automatic? When you turn thirteen, you're expected to observe the commandments and be a good Jew. The ceremony and the elaborate parties afterward are not required. The spectacle of it, the whole huge singing in the synagogue and having a big expensive party element, is new. Or contemporary, anyway. Mid-century. Like the suburbs."

Rickie laughed. She knew that the bar mitzvah ritual was about being a man, but she didn't know that the big tsimmes wasn't required. She could see how not having the ceremony and party would have been a big disappointment, but they were still considered to be nice Jewish men, once they turned thirteen: Marty, Kenny, Jimmy, and CJ. Nobody seemed to worry too much if Eileen was disappointed or if girls in Monticello, New York, even had bat mitzvah parties in the 1940s. She would have turned thirteen in 1944, when it was no longer possible to look away from the specter of the Holocaust. A few years later, she was dead.

The headshrinkers and analysts in the family most certainly had their theories about Eileen and her death as the worst thing to happen to the family after they'd all turned thirteen with no bar mitzvah. At some point, Rickie had heard all the Jackson relatives she knew espouse a theory about Eileen's death. Some people said it was pure narcissism that drove her to refuse the amputation, but what good-looking twenty-one-year-old woman would want to have her leg hacked off? It wasn't just that one-leggedness would have made her ugly. Rickie was sure that Eileen was a lot smarter than that. She didn't want what the doctors were offering: butchery. There were no guarantees that the amputation would remove all the cancer, so why bother?

In the same way, the relatives told the story of how Eileen married Hal Schlozman and then dropped dead—as if she were in denial or as if she hoped that somehow getting married would get rid of the cancer. Rickie didn't think that was right, either. Another version was this: Eileen kept her leg, married her sweetheart, and then had a sudden, catastrophic decline. She didn't linger on and on in agony; she just died—with her leg and her dignity still attached. Rickie admired that. Eileen, she figured, was like Ethel Rosenberg, sticking to her story. In the end, Eileen probably suffered a lot less than Ethel did. Eileen was her own person, all the way to the end of her short life.

Cousin Becky Jackson came up and joined the conversation.

"You know," Rickie told Becky. "Esti has been telling me about the family, and I've been interested in the ancestors and all this family history, and now I need a descendant to name as the beneficiary of this descendants trust that CJ and Annie created for me and Tom."

"Rickie" she said. "Are you going to have a baby?"

"No, no," she said. "I really don't think that is going to happen. But you're a parent."

"True."

"And I need a descendant. So what I'm thinking is that Charlie can be the descendant in charge of the trust and the ancestors."

"Charlie. As in my son, Charles Martin Wilson Jackson?"

Rickie laughed and nodded. "That's exactly the Charlie I mean! He likes stories and books already, and you and Sue already have him in Hebrew school, right?"

"Right."

"And when he's thirteen, he'll have a big-ass bar mitzvah?"

"That's the plan."

"So," Rickie continued. "The perfect nice little Jewish boy, created from an anonymous Jewish donor, a half-Jewish mom, and a whole big tree of ancestors holding him up, will become a one hundred percent, full-on, bar mitzvah-ed Jewish man!" She stopped and gave a huge exhale. "It almost makes up for the centuries of pogroms and Ukrainians and Germans and Poles chasing our family out of the country and killing the ones who couldn't leave."

"That's a bit stark," Becky said. "But I take your point."

"Not to lay too big of a burden on Charlie or anything," Rickie said. "And don't get me wrong. If Charlie had been a girl, I'd have made her the descendant trustee. But things being as they are, he's the perfect choice."

•

AT THE END OF the day, Rickie was bone-tired. She'd heard grief could do that, and all the paperwork and conversations, on top of hospital visits, worrying, and phone calls, had worn her out. Before she left to catch a flight back to Minneapolis, Deborah Walker invited Rickie to come with her to Binghamton for some alumni meeting and then drive up to Rochester, make a quick stop on a consulting trip, and then fly back to Minneapolis from Buffalo. Rickie was slow to move.

"It's still summer," Deborah said. "We'll do a road trip. It's perfect."

"I know," Rickie said. "But I have to rest and do some prep for my fall classes."

"Do it on the plane," she said. "Or in the car. We'll fly into LaGuardia and drive up to Binghamton. Then we'll drive to Rochester for my meeting and fly out of Buffalo. Don't you have family there?"

"Well, traces of them, anyway, in Monticello and Rochester. The only relatives left in Rochester are my grandmother and my aunt. They're dead and buried there." Rickie paused. "I guess I do want to visit Rochester, see where they all lived, visit the cemetery. I mean, I pay the bill for the upkeep now. They all think I'm a nice Jewish girl and a good daughter"

Deborah looked at Rickie and smiled. "You are," she said. "Where are they buried?"

"Mount Hope Cemetery," she said. "It doesn't sound very Jewish to me."

Deborah pulled a guidebook from the trunk of her car. "Hmmm," she said. "Check this out. This section on Rochester says that Mount Hope Cemetery is one of the finest Victorian municipal cemeteries in the US. All kinds of famous people are buried there. Susan B. Anthony. Frederick Douglass. Cool." She paused. "Seriously, Rickie Lynn. I think it's worth the trip. All you need to do is buy your plane ticket. My consulting gig will cover the rest."

Rickie considered the offer. Back in the Park Avenue duplex in Minneapolis, the next-door neighbor had gone to Finland a couple years ago and tracked down some distant relatives. They had a blast together, and now the neighbor was making regular visits to the homeland. Rickie had no reason to go all the way back to Poland or the Ukraine. The old folks who'd stayed behind had probably died in the gas chambers or the killing fields. It wasn't likely she'd find a trace of any relative in Dubno or Dnepropetrovsk. Instead, her family inscriptions were in American places: Topeka, Monticello, Rochester. Mount Hope Cemetery was beckoning her. Finally, she scowled and then nodded and smiled at Deborah. "OK, OK," she said. "I'll go!"

13

The office at Mount Hope Cemetery could have been a ranger station or a tiny library in a small town.

"Is it closed?" Rickie said. "Whoever heard of a closed cemetery?"

"Is this a Christian cemetery?" Deborah Walker asked as she parked the rental car.

"I don't think so," Rickie said. "As you may recall, we came here to find my Jewish relatives."

"OK, OK."

"Let me see what's what," Rickie said. She felt this horrible flush of realization bordering on utter, abject despair that she might not be able to find her relatives, which was the reason she had wanted to visit Mount Hope Cemetery in Rochester, New York, in the first place. Then she spotted a sheaf of maps in a plastic box next to the office door.

She got out, grabbed a map, and returned to the car. "Here's a map," she said. "Do you think it'll help at all?"

"Yes," Deborah said and took the map. She was a consultant, after all, and was good at solving problems. "Jews are buried with their congregations. Yes. Here's Temple Beth El. Here's Beth Shalom. Here's Sinai. What's the name of their congregation?"

Rickie shrugged.

"Look," she said to the map. "I see a bunch of congregations in this section. Should we start there? I think we can find them."

Outside, the sky was steel gray, and the leaves were mostly

off the trees. Tree branches stuck out here and there, pointing black arms and fingers in all directions.

"What are their names again?" Deborah asked.

"Leah Grossman Jackson," Rickie said. "That's my grandmother. And Eileen Virginia Jackson Schlozman is my aunt."

Deborah gaped. "Her name is really Eileen Virginia? I thought that was a joke."

"I've already told you I don't know why my grandmother picked those *goyische* names," Rickie said. "They all looked Jewish. Sort of. I mean, most of the people on that side of the family have the usual dark hair and eyes. In the photographs I've seen, my grandmother looks a little like Ethel Rosenberg. And then there are the ones with fair hair and hazel eyes, such as my grandfather."

Deborah nodded. "That's what comes from mixing with Poles and Ukrainians and Germans."

They got out of the car and started walking up and down the rows of Rickie's people, or half of them, anyway: Kleins, Joffes, Cohens, Horowitzes, Goldmans, Kuretskys.

Nearby, a big party of crows occupied a tree just past the rental car. They were the loudest crows she'd ever heard.

"A group of crows is called a murder," she said out loud. It was as if she'd just exhaled a little breath of information she'd learned in an undergraduate lit seminar at Binghamton.

The noise was viscous. She recalled again that CJ used to say that he didn't get into Phi Beta Kappa because his grades were terrible during his sophomore year at the University of Rochester.

"My sister died of cancer," he mourned. "And my mother was up all night screaming and crying. I couldn't think."

The murderous crows hollered as she walked past one headstone, two. She tried to think. Then she spotted the word

Virginia. On top of the headstone was a Star of David and beneath it, in big capital letters, was "Schlozman." Below it, in a flower-festooned rectangle, were the words she had been seeking: "Eileen Virginia. 1931-1952. Beloved wife and daughter."

"Hey," Rickie yelled to Deborah Walker. She sounded strangled, as if a crow were stuck in her throat. "I found Eileen."

"Fantastic," she said. "I bet your grandmother is nearby."

Two rows south and three headstones east of Eileen, Rickie stopped again, for there she was. "Beloved Mother'," she shouted. "It sounds like a curse. 'Leah G. Jackson. 1898-1967'!"

•

DEBORAH JOINED RICKIE as she finished taking cheap-camera photos of the headstones. "The crows are deafening," she said.

"I know," Rickie said.

Deborah pulled out a folder. "Let's say *Kaddish* for your aunt and grandmother," she said. "I've got it here in this folder. When I give you a signal, you say 'Amen.'"

"Wait," Rickie said. "I should say something to my relatives, so they'll recognize me."

"Aren't you always singing some family song about a candy store?" Deborah asked.

"Yes!" Rickie said. "It's to the tune of 'HaTikvah,' in a Yiddish accent. Follow along: 'Once I had a candy store. Business was so bad. I asked mein wife what to do. This is what she said: Take a bissel kerosene. Schmear it on the floor. Take a match. Give a scratch. Fwee! No more candy store!'"

Rickie made big arm circles. The murder of crows went wild. Deborah Walker cleared her throat. It was time to say *Kaddish* and find their way home.

•

ACROSS THE STREET FROM Mount Hope Cemetery was a

little strip mall featuring a sandwich shop, a copy shop, and a Dunkin' Donuts.

"After all this," Rickie said. "I want a jelly donut."

"It looks closed. How about a sandwich?" Deborah suggested. She pulled into the parking lot.

They got out of the car, and the crows were still *kvetching*. "Can you hear that?" Rickie said. "Those crows?"

"They're crazy," Deborah said. She headed for the sandwich shop.

"Do you really want that?" Rickie asked her. She fidgeted and looked at the dark and empty Dunkin' Donuts.

Deborah paused and surveyed Rickie. "Yes. It's OK," she said. "We have time." She went in the sandwich shop.

Rickie Jackson lingered in the parking lot. She was nervous about the drive to Buffalo, the car rental return, the security line at the airport, boarding the plane for the last flight of the day from Buffalo to Minneapolis. She wanted to go home. She inhaled hard through her nose and watched the guy behind the counter assembling Deborah's sandwich. Then she turned to regard the cemetery and its cacophonous crows.

"I still want a jelly donut," she said when Deborah came out with her sandwich in a bag.

"Come on," she said.

Deborah drove. Rickie exhaled and shut her eyes. Her head was full of cacophony and murder and the miserable noise of crying, screaming Leah trying to save her daughter and sad, angry CJ trying to study, and frustrated and freaked out Uncle Marty trying to get his mentors at the medical school to help his sister, and Uncle Jimmy and Uncle Kenny who had fled for college at Ithaca and Buffalo, and her wandering grandfather, Sol, who was somewhere nearby but not at home with the rest of the family, and her young, dying aunt.

She wondered about her grandmother Leah, if she had been scared and furious as she fled across the top of Poland and Germany to Bremerhaven, where she caught a ship to Ellis Island and then boarded a train all the way the hell out to Topeka, Kansas. And then all the way back to New York with five kids? She imagined that they must have had a very long train trip. Leah could not have been calm. Rickie bet she yelled at those kids. She bet the kids fought with each other. She bet all of them were bored and terrified.

At some point, probably on the plane, Deborah Walker, a person who was always interested in measuring results, was going to ask Rickie how she felt about all this family history of grief and loss. Rickie hoped she would remember to thank Deborah for planning the trip and figuring out the cemetery and saying *Kaddish* and singing the "HaTikvah" candy store song. Rickie figured she'd tell Deborah that she felt closer to all of them, the Jackson relatives she never really knew. But of course she knew them: they were exactly like her.

•

"WE NEED TO STOP for gas," Deborah said as they approached the exit for the airport at Buffalo. "I see a gas station."

Rickie got out of the car, fiddled with the gas pump, and looked at the pinks, yellows, dark blues, and grays layering the horizon. She'd driven through this part of New York before, but she'd never lived here nor even spent much time here before this trip. Still, it did not feel strange to her. Her family was here. Her relatives were in the ground, nearby. The gas pumped chugged, thumped, and stopped. She replaced the nozzle, screwed in the gas cap, went inside to pay. She was leaving a familiar place and going home.

In Buffalo, travelers dropped off rental cars in a ramp and then crossed the street, waited in line, and checked in the car at the main desk. It seemed like a big *megillah*. Rickie preferred airports that direct people to drive over those tire spikes, leave the keys in the car, and get the hell out of there.

Deborah Walker had to make a work call, so she found a phone booth near the baggage claim, and Rickie got in line to return the car. In front of her was a woman who looked to be about Rickie's age, maybe a little bit older. She smiled at Rickie and jiggled her keys.

"Coming or going?" she asked.

Rickie gaped at her for a second. "Returning a car," she said. "Going."

"Me, too," she said. "Just finished a road trip."

Sometimes those kinds of random conversations were just the result of people flirting out of sheer boredom, but Rickie was feeling that this woman was actually earnest, as if she really had something to say, as if she were a messenger doing her job.

She looked at Rickie and continued. "I flew into LaGuardia and spent a few days with a friend in Westchester. Then I drove up Route 17."

"Through Binghamton?"

She brightened. "Yes," she said. "I went through Binghamton."

"I was just there. I went to SUNY-Binghamton," Rickie said. "In the 80s."

"Crazy," she said. "I was there then, too."

"Did you stop at the Roscoe Diner?"

"Of course I did!"

"Yes," Rickie said. "I used to stop at the diner in Monticello." She was about to tell her that CJ, her dad, had grown up there, and she always got a kick out of visiting his old haunts, but her voice caught.

"I drove straight through this time," the woman said. "I wanted to get up to Ithaca."

Rickie nodded.

"I actually went to grad school in Ithaca. So I stopped for the night there and then went on to Rochester and now Buffalo." She paused. "Not very glamourous."

Rickie shrugged. "It's good to see friends. I haven't been out this way in years."

"I know!" she said. "I used to make this trip all the time." She paused, glanced at the counter, and pushed her luggage forward. The line was moving. "When I was younger, I had a boyfriend in Rochester, and we'd drive up here from Binghamton or Ithaca, and it was just no big deal. Snow, rain, whatever. We never thought anything would happen." She paused again and looked at Rickie. "But now he's gone, and my parents are gone, and so are other people around me. Now I know things happen."

It was her turn at the counter. As she moved to take her turn, Rickie remembered a different trip to New York, when she was younger and never thought anything would happen.

She'd found a cheap flight to Newark and thought it might be fun to see what Terry Scalco, her on-and-off girlfriend, was up to. Then she was going to catch a Short Line Bus up to Binghamton to see her buddy Chris Calabrese defend his dissertation on Shelley. Her plan fell apart the minute she landed and Terry Scalco was nowhere in sight. She sat in the Newark airport until Terry Scalco finally paged her. Terry told Rickie that her car had died, and Rickie should take a PATH train or a bus into the City and then take the LIRR out to Port Jefferson, Long Island.

"You can take a cab to my house from there," she said. "It's not that far."

Rickie was thinking she'd just take a bus from the airport in Newark to Port Authority in New York City and take the

Short Line bus from there to Binghamton and forget about Terry Scalco once and for all. Instead, she told herself she could go visit Terry and then come back to the City and catch a bus up to see Chris maybe that day, maybe later. That plan vanished as it took pretty much the rest of the day to get to Terry's little rental house way the hell out on Long Island.

When Rickie knocked on Terry Scalco's door, Terry looked at Rickie, smiled, and said, "I forgot how cute you are."

Terry Scalco was the first cocaine addict Rickie had ever known, but now that she'd graduated from college and was trying to build a clientele as a personal trainer while she was studying for the LSAT and applying to law schools, she seemed to be less of a cokehead and more of a plain old drunk. In her freezer was a gigantic bottle of Tanqueray, the size of a small, green person. They started in on it about three seconds after Rickie had come inside and dropped her bag.

Terry Scalco still had that cokehead bad temper, so in the late morning of the next day, when there was clearly no way Rickie was going make it upstate and did not want to spend one more second with Terry Scalco, she called this woman named Jane Dixon, a friend of Deborah Walker's in Minneapolis.

"I'm at work," Jane Dixon said. "Come by. I'll give you the key to my apartment, and you can drop off your stuff. We'll meet up later and go out."

The second after Rickie had hung up the phone with Jane Dixon, Terry's roommate, Andy, who had also been at SUNY-Binghamton, walked into the kitchen.

"Would you mind dropping me off at the train station on your way to work?" Rickie asked him.

"Not if you can be ready in fifteen minutes," he said.

"You don't want to stay one more day?" Terry asked Rickie

as she was packing up her duffel bag. Terry was looking out the window at her dead car as she was talking to Rickie.

Rickie shook her head. "I'm not even supposed to be here anyway," she said. "I didn't call Chris. Now it's too late."

"What are you going to do?"

"I've got a seven-thirty flight out of Newark tomorrow morning," Rickie said as she zipped her bag. "I was thinking I'd go into the City and stay with this friend of Deborah Walker's. The friend lives in the East Village now, and it'll be easier to get to the airport."

Terry looked at Rickie, raised an eyebrow, and looked back at her car. "A friend from Minneapolis? In the East Village?"

Rickie hedged. "Friend of a friend," she said.

"Fuck you," Terry Scalco replied.

Rickie said good-bye to the couch where Terry Scalco and her green bottle were smoking a cigarette. Terry didn't even look at Rickie. Rickie walked out the door and got into the car with Andy.

It seemed like she was back in the City in no time, and Jane Dixon's workplace was about halfway between her East Village apartment and Penn Station. Rickie picked up the key to Jane's apartment and started walking.

On the way to Jane Dixon's apartment, Rickie stopped at a shoe store and got some black leather high tops. Then she went into a clothes store where she got a long-sleeved T-shirt, red on one side and black on the other. Her last stop was Astor Place Barbers, where she got a sharp, short haircut. Then she dropped off her duffel bag at Jane Dixon's, took a shower in this tiny little stall rigged up in what was once a kitchen pantry, and went out again. She thought she might go see the Statue of Liberty, but instead, a girl in a storefront bar smiled at her, and she ducked inside and joined her.

By the time she met up with Jane at about midnight, Rickie Jackson was almost a completely different person. Jane and Rickie went to the World, in Alphabet City, and they stayed out until it was time for Rickie to grab her bag and take the subway to the bus to the plane out of Newark.

She got back to Minneapolis in that limbo state between still drunk and hung over, and it seemed that nobody in the Park Avenue duplex was particularly glad to see her. She said she'd been out with Jane Dixon, but she decided not to tell anybody that in all the commotion, she'd missed the trip to Binghamton, gotten drunk and fell into bed with Terry Scalco, and then made out with a stranger in the bathroom of a storefront bar. She didn't really like being a liar about it, but she also doubted that telling everything would have made much of a difference. She managed to apologize and make it up to Chris Calabrese by going to his wedding in Elmira, New York the following spring. Chris and Rickie stayed friends, but she and Terry Scalco did not.

●

AT THE RENTAL CAR return counter, the woman who knew better than Rickie did was gone. It struck Rickie that the woman was right. She'd just been lucky. It does happen. A friend dies. You blow off a really good friend and get messed up with some bad-tempered ex-girlfriend. You get some awful virus from a stranger. You go to meet somebody who doesn't show up. You oversleep, miss the train, the bus, the plane. First one parent dies, then the other. You worry that you've missed all the connections you could or should have made in your life. You are as good as dead.

Earlier that day, in her last dream before she woke up in the Rochester hotel room, her brother Tom was telling her this horrible news.

"Nicole is suing you for a hundred and twenty-five thousand dollars," he said.

"Nicole who?" Rickie said. "What for?"

"Child support. She's taking you to the cleaners."

She'd returned to consciousness as if swimming up from the muddy bottom of one of those man-made lakes in Kansas. She had never, ever had an unsupported child or a girlfriend named Nicole. Even so, Nicole was taking her to the cleaners, and she was terrified.

Rickie didn't say anything to Deborah about the dream, but she felt uneasy and could hardly look at her. On the road between the Holiday Inn where they'd spent the night and Mount Hope Cemetery, where they were going to visit her relatives and say *Kaddish*, Deborah wanted to talk about her relationship with Cricket.

"We're going to be together," she was saying, "So Cricket can be a member at my synagogue."

"She can be a member just because you are?"

"Yes," she said. "Spouses and domestic partners of members are automatically included."

"Even if the spouses and domestic partners aren't Jewish?"

"Even so," she said. "We're inclusive."

Rickie shifted in her seat. "The Jewish kids I've known were always telling me that Jews don't recruit," she said. "How can somebody who's not even officially Jewish be a member of a synagogue? Can anybody at your synagogue just decide to be Jewish?"

"I told you. We're inclusive."

"OK, but if you include anybody and everybody, then what's the point? How is that even a synagogue? Sounds more like a pot-luck."

"A person could always convert if she really wanted to be official."

"Convert? You mean go to Hebrew school and all that? Get a bar mitzvah?"

"If Cricket, for example, or even you, wanted a bat mitzvah, there are Hebrew classes," she said. "Hebrew school's not just for kids."

Rickie laughed, but it was a queasy laugh. If she said out loud that she did not want to join her synagogue, convert, or get a bat mitzvah, Deborah would say she was being contrary, but that was exactly how Rickie felt. Back in Kansas, when Rickie was in seventh grade, all of a sudden it seemed that every week somebody was having a bar or bat mitzvah. CJ would always say that it really wasn't up to a rabbi to decide that on one particular day you are a man, not a mouse. Then they'd talk about something else.

"You know," Rickie said to Deborah Walker. "It really stuck in CJ's craw that he never had a bar mitzvah, and my cousin Esti told me that one of the many things that her dad, Uncle Marty, was pissed off about was that he never had a bar mitzvah. Esti said that Marty stopped going to *shul*, stopped telling people he was Jewish, and married my aunt Frances. A *shiksa*! He didn't want Becky or Esti to be Jewish at all."

"And what about your dad?" Deborah said.

Rickie shrugged. "You know that story. CJ married a *shiksa*, too. But actually, Annie became just as Jewish as CJ. She cooked all the special foods and bought a Passover plate from a Jewish potter she knew. She wasn't really interested in the religious parts, but she had the cultural Judaism down cold."

"What about your aunt, the *shiksa*?"

"Aunt Frances? The analyst?" Rickie said. "She didn't seem

like she was ever interested in any kind of Judaism. Still, you can't say it doesn't mean anything that she and Uncle Marty's two daughters are named Rebecca and Esther. There's a reason why they aren't named Susie and Kathy, right?"

"Not so sure," Deborah said. "What about their sister, your aunt? Eileen Virginia? That's a *shiksa* name, and she wasn't one!"

"OK," Rickie said. "But still. There's something about being Jewish that is right down in your marrow, in your DNA. You can call your kids Bobby or Eileen or Rebecca or Esther."

"Or Rickie or Tom."

She nodded. "That's what I'm saying. Rickie or Tom or Rebecca or Charles or Shlomo or Rivka or Itzhak. You can dress British, but you think Yiddish, right? It's in you."

"Essentialism," Deborah Walker scoffed. "Are you saying there's an essential Jew? All converts are not Jewish because they lack this essence of Judaism, whatever it is?"

Rickie pressed her feet into the floorboard. "You can say what you want," she said. "But I'm more Jewish than half your congregation. I'm just not quite kosher."

•

FROM THE RENTAL CAR area, Rickie could see that Deborah was finishing her call and hanging up the phone. She looked at Rickie, at first as if she didn't recognize her and then as if she thought Rickie were somebody else—maybe Cricket, maybe some old girlfriend, maybe somebody out of a dream.

As Deborah approached, Rickie inhaled and waited for her to scowl and then drop some bad news bomb. Instead, she gave Rickie a mild look and said, in reasonable tones, "Let's go."

They took an escalator upstairs, and Rickie braced herself for security. In Minneapolis, the officer at the screening site had apparently not liked Rickie's looks. The officer was solid and buzz-cut neat, packed into his navy-blue uniform. He kept asking Rickie if everything was out of her pockets.

Rickie said, "Yes," and then she reached for the boarding pass she'd stuck in her back pocket.

The security officer flinched, as if Rickie were drawing a concealed Magnum. He made Rickie put her boarding pass in a little basket. Then he made her go through the special full-body scanner. It looked like a giant version of those pneumatic tubes in the the pharmacy at KU Medical Center.

"Stand facing your belongings," snapped another navy-clad bureaucratic bouncer.

Everything paused. Rickie held her breath and waited for somebody to slap the cuffs on her wrists. She'd get interrogated. They'd torture her. Not nearly as brave as Ethel Rosenberg nor as stubborn as Julius, she'd confess to some crime she'd never even dreamed of committing. She was on her way to prison. Then the security tube blinked. She exhaled. The dark blue bouncer waved her through.

Now, at the Buffalo airport, Rickie followed Deborah Walker off the escalator. There was no line at the security check in. The bouncer-in-blue at the security desk had thick, dark hair and dark eyes, like Esti, Becky, CJ, Marty, Jimmy, Kenny, Leah, Eileen, Tom, and Rickie herself. He took Rickie's boarding pass and her ID, sized her up, paused as if to get a whiff of her, and waved her through. He barely looked at Deborah Walker.

They collected their bags and belongings, and Rickie leaned on the end rail of the security area to zip her ID into her backpack. As she hucked on the backpack, she happened to look past the security apparatus toward the wide concourse. There, tucked in the wall between a hot dog joint and a newsstand, was a familiar array of orange and pink block letters.

"Hey, Rickie," Deborah Walker said. "What do I see?"

"Dunkin' Donuts," Rickie said. "I'm in Paradise."

ACKNOWLEDGMENTS

Suburban Heathens began as a NaNoWriMo project, and many people and institutions have helped in its metamorphosis. First, thanks to Jonis Agee and Brent Spencer for their encouragement and support. I am also grateful for the college and grad school friends and teachers, near and far, who have backed me for many years. Julie Daniels and Lynette D'Amico provided editorial help, and the members of Bertha, the legendary writing group, delivered essential feedback and camaraderie. Also, my colleagues and students at Inver Hills Community College have fostered a much appreciated teaching/learning environment. Thanks to Jane, my daughter; Jack, Maggi, and Amy, my siblings, Paul and Sue, my siblings in-law; Erin, Lindsey, and Jessi, my nieces, and my cousins, Karen, Dorrie, Susie, and Patrick for contributing memories and enhancing rumors and speculations, and to Michele Steinwald for her good eye. Finally, *Suburban Heathens* is dedicated to Mitchell Toney, my longtime artistic conscience, and to my dad, Lester L. Lansky, MD. May their memory be for a blessing.

ABOUT THE AUTHOR

ELLEN LANSKY has published several short stories in local, regional, and national publications. Her novella *Harmonic Convergence* was the runner-up in *Evergreen Chronicles'* first national novella contest. Her first novel, *Golden Jeep,* appeared in 2011. In addition, she has published articles about Ernest Hemingway, Djuna Barnes, Paul and Jane Bowles, Dorothy Parker, Katherine Anne Porter, F. Scott and Zelda Fitzgerald, Tennessee Williams, and Carson McCullers in several anthologies and journals, including *Literature and Medicine* and *Dionysos.* Her essay "Under the Covers with Melissa Etheridge" appeared in *Singing for Themselves: Essays on Women in Popular Music.* Her most recent scholarly essay is "Trashed: Women Under the Influence of Alcohol in Wright's Native Son" for *Southern Comforts: Alcohol and Drinking in the US South.* She attended St. Catherine University (BA), Binghamton University (MA), and the University of Minnesota (PhD). She lives in Minneapolis and teaches literature, composition, and creative writing at Inver Hills Community College.

www.ingramcontent.com/pod-product-compliance
Lightning Source LLC
Chambersburg PA
CBHW032035180726

48284CB00008B/2591